I0835613

Machen Society
PRESS

Walnut Lodge

L. Chambers Wright

ISBN: 978-1-967310-46-3

Machen Society Press
11876 Stanley Valley Road
Gate City, Virginia 24251
Contact: Publisher@MachenSocietyPress.com
Website: http://MachenSocietyPress.com

Printed in the U.S.A.

Chapter 1

He didn't trust the sapling. Its thin trunk bent hard beneath his weight, leaves trembling in the mountain wind like they knew what was coming. Still, the alternative lay a hundred feet below him in a graveyard of jagged stone. He wrapped both hands around the trunk and hauled himself upward.

The sapling snapped with a sharp crack. For one suspended second, he hung there in silence. Then the mountain gave way beneath him.

His boots tore through wet leaves and loose soil. One ankle twisted violently. Pain flared white-hot up his leg, and gravity took over before he could recover. He slammed sideways into the slope and began sliding down the mountainside in a helpless tumble.

It wasn't a clean fall. That would have been merciful. This was slower. Meaner. The steep incline carried him like a body dumped into floodwater. Damp leaves slicked the ground like black ice, and every frantic attempt to stop himself only sent him spinning harder.

Mud smeared across his jacket. Sharp branches whipped against his face and arms. He clawed desperately at the earth, fingers digging through wet rot and moss, but the mountain offered nothing solid to hold.

A root slammed into his ribs hard enough to steal his breath. Another branch raked across his cheek. He caught sight of gray sky flashing between the treetops before the world flipped again into dirt, bark, and dead leaves.

"God—!"

The curse vanished into a grunt as he crashed against a jagged shelf of stone. Pain exploded through his lower back and hip. He tried grabbing two young oaks growing from the slope, but the thin trunks bent like reeds beneath his weight. One tore free of the ground entirely, roots dangling in the air as he continued sliding.

The mountain seemed endless. Twigs snapped beneath him. Stones skipped into darkness below. His shoulder struck another rock hard enough to numb his entire arm. Panic rose hot in his chest now, raw and primal. Not fear of injury. Fear of momentum. Fear that he couldn't stop. Fear that the mountain had already decided where he belonged.

At last his body slammed onto a narrow rocky ledge with enough force to rattle his teeth. He skidded several more inches before stopping abruptly against a cluster of thorny brush clinging to the cliffside.

Silence rushed in around him. He lay there gasping, staring up through the black lattice of tree branches overhead. Every inch of him burned. His palms felt flayed raw. One knee throbbed violently beneath torn denim. Warm blood trickled down the side of his neck where something sharp had opened the skin.

For several long seconds, he couldn't move at all. Then pain returned in full. He groaned and rolled onto his side, clutching at his ribs as nausea twisted through his stomach. Something in his lower back screamed in protest. His kidney felt like it had been hit with a sledgehammer.

"Jesus Christ…" The words came out hoarse and shaking. Slowly, he pushed himself upright. That was when he looked over the edge. The breath froze in his lungs.

Far below him, jagged gray rocks jutted from the mountainside like broken teeth. The drop disappeared into darkness and pine shadow, deep enough that the trees beneath looked miniature.

Samson's Cliff. His stomach dropped harder than his body had. Everybody around Roan Mountain knew Samson's Cliff. Hikers slipped there every few years. Tourists underestimated the terrain, leaned too far over wet stone for a photograph, or wandered too close after dark. Rescue crews sometimes recovered bodies days later from the ravine below.

Sometimes they didn't. The mountain kept what it wanted. He stared at the drop, heart hammering wildly against bruised ribs. Another few feet. One more broken branch. One more bounce down the slope. That would have been it.

No dramatic final words. No rescue helicopter sweeping overhead. Just another corpse at the bottom of the mountain for somebody else to find. Or not find.

Cold wind curled across the cliffside and slipped beneath his jacket. He backed away from the edge immediately, hands trembling hard enough he could barely steady himself. His pulse roared in his ears. The icy air carried the scent of wet pine, moss, and distant rain.

Stupid. The word came quick and merciless. *Stupid to hike alone.* But he hadn't exactly had options anymore.

The trip had collapsed piece by piece before he ever reached the mountain. First Greg canceled because of some business emergency back in Knoxville. Then Aaron suddenly had "family obligations." Finally Leigh backed out two days before the trip with another excuse involving her sister.

Her sister always seemed to be dying. Cancer. Lupus. Heart trouble. Now end-stage diabetes. Yet, strangely, with all the terminal illnesses, she didn't require a hospital or hospice. Just rest at home. The excuses blurred together after a while.

At first he'd believed every one of them. Leigh cried easily when she lied. That made her convincing. But eventually even grief became repetitive. Same vague details. Same sudden emergencies that conveniently appeared whenever they had plans together.

This time he'd checked. He'd called Stacy himself. Not accusingly. Not angrily. Just concern. A quick phone call to wish her well after Leigh told him she was barely hanging on after complications from pregnancy. Except Stacy wasn't sick. Wasn't diabetic either.

She'd sounded confused more than anything. Tired from caring for a newborn, yes, but otherwise healthy. Back at work already. She even laughed awkwardly at one point and said, "Honestly, I hardly see Leigh anymore. I thought she was usually off traveling somewhere with you."

That had been the moment something cold settled permanently into his stomach. He never confronted Leigh afterward. Not yet. Didn't see the point. People who wanted to stay found reasons to stay. People looking for exits invented funerals and illnesses.

The cabin reservation had already been paid for anyway, non-refundable, buried deep in the mountains where cell service barely existed. He'd decided to come alone rather than waste the trip. Maybe the solitude would clear his head. Roan Mountain always had before. He could confront her while in control of his emotions.

Roan Mountain had mattered to him since childhood. His father used to bring him here every October when the leaves turned bronze and gold. They'd hike the ridges together in heavy flannel jackets while fog rolled through the valleys below like drifting oceans. Back then the mountains felt ancient but comforting, enormous but alive in a protective way.

Today they felt indifferent. Cruel, even. He spat blood onto the rocks beside him and slowly forced himself to stand. Every muscle in his body protested the motion. His left ankle held, though pain stabbed through it the moment he put full weight down. Probably sprained. Maybe worse. The realization settled over him quietly. If he'd broken something up here, nobody would know for days.

He reached instinctively for his pocket. His phone was still there. Thank God. But he didn't pull it out yet. If the screen was shattered or the battery dead, he didn't want to know while balanced beside a cliff. One problem at a time.

He turned carefully and examined the narrow ledge stretching ahead of him. The slope above looked impossible now. Wet leaves still slid steadily downward in little trickles around exposed roots and loose stones. Trying to climb back the way he came would be suicide.

Forward was the only option. Carefully, he began moving along the ridge. The terrain narrowed in places until only a few feet separated him from open air. Thick briars crowded the path. Low branches clawed at his jacket and scraped his arms. Several times loose gravel shifted beneath his boots and sent fresh jolts of adrenaline through him.

He kept moving anyway. The mountain grew darker around him as evening settled deeper through the trees. Wind hissed softly through pine needles overhead. Somewhere far below, water rushed unseen through the ravine.

Then he noticed the light. At first it was so faint he thought it might be another hiker's flashlight moving through the woods below. Another light appeared. Then another. Warm amber pinpricks shimmered between the trees ahead, flickering softly through the fog-dark forest.

He frowned. Nobody lived up here. The Appalachian Trail crossed parts of the mountain, sure, but there were no homes this deep inside protected land. No lodges. No private cabins. Certainly nothing with electricity. Yet as he moved forward, the lights multiplied.

Dozens of them now. His pace slowed. The trees thinned abruptly along the ridge. The structure beyond them finally emerged from the darkness. His breath caught.

The building sprawled across the mountainside like something torn from another century and abandoned among the wilderness. Tall windows blazed gold against the blue-gray dusk. Multiple stories rose behind massive stone walls. Towers and steep gables climbed above the tree line. Shadows moved faintly behind curtains.

Not a cabin. Not a ranger station. A mansion. An enormous one. His skin prickled instantly. That wasn't possible. No road led up here. No construction crews could've hauled material this deep into the preserve without everybody in region hearing about it. The state barely allowed new signage along some of the trails, much less a structure this size. And yet it stood there fully lit, silent and waiting among the trees.

Wind stirred again. For just a moment, he thought he heard music drifting faintly from somewhere inside. Piano keys. Slow. Uneven. Ancient. Every instinct told him something about the place was wrong. But the cold begun sinking through his clothes now. Darkness gathered fast across the mountain. His side throbbed with every breath. Blood dried sticky against his neck.

Whatever waited inside those walls was going to be much better than freezing to death on the ridge. So despite the growing knot of dread in his stomach, he stepped toward the mansion.

Chapter 2

The structure looming beyond the trees wasn't just large. It was monstrous. A sprawling fortress of black timber and dark stone rose from the mountainside like something transplanted from another century.

Four towering stories climbed into the evening sky beneath steep cathedral-like gables roofed in weather-darkened slate. Golden light spilled from dozens upon dozens of tall windows, glowing through the fog like suspended lanterns. Against the deepening blue of dusk, the entire place looked unreal, less constructed than conjured.

He stood frozen at the edge of the tree line, chest still heaving from the climb along the ridge. That hadn't been there before. Not possible. He'd hiked Walnut Hill less than a year ago. The trails had been untouched then, nothing but dense forest, exposed stone, and stretches of rhododendron thick enough to swallow the path.

Roan Mountain land management barely allowed maintenance crews to widen footbridges without environmental hearings. A structure this size would have required blasting roads through protected forest. Everybody in Carter County would've known. Hell, everybody in East Tennessee would've known. Yet there it stood in absolute silence, immense and immovable beneath the mountains.

The deeper he stared, the stranger the lodge became. Wide wings branched outward from the main structure like the arms of some enormous château. Turrets rose from the corners. Massive stone chimneys exhaled lazy streams of smoke into the cold air above the trees. Warm amber light flickered behind stained-glass windows high along the upper floors.

Beautiful. But wrong. The mountain around it seemed almost dimmer somehow, swallowed beneath its glow. He moved forward carefully, limping now as adrenaline faded and pain settled into his body with growing persistence. His ribs throbbed every time he inhaled. One ankle pulsed with sharp little stabs beneath his weight. Blood had dried stiff against both hands where branches and stone had opened the skin.

The incline eased as he approached the clearing, but his legs still trembled from exhaustion. Up close, the scale of the place became overwhelming. Stone retaining walls terraced down the hillside. Iron lanterns lined a massive gravel drive wide enough for several carriages abreast.

He slowed. Carriages. Not replicas. Real ones. Glossy black lacquer gleamed beneath the lantern light as drivers helped elegantly dressed guests onto a long crimson carpet stretching toward the entrance. Horses stamped clouds of steam into the cold air while polished vintage automobiles rolled slowly through the circular drive behind them. Men in tuxedos laughed beneath silk masks. Women draped in velvet and satin climbed marble steps beneath towering arches.

Music drifted faintly from somewhere inside. Strings. Piano. The low hum of conversation. "Hello, sir."

He jumped hard enough pain shot through his ribs. A young man stood a few feet behind him. He wore a pressed white shirt beneath a dark vest and black slacks. Freckles covered his pale face. His bright red hair looked neatly combed despite the mountain wind, and he wore the easy smile of someone entirely at home here.

"Sorry," the young man said quickly. "Didn't mean to scare you."

He stared at him for a moment, catching his breath.

"You all right there?" the boy asked, eyes drifting across Tyler's muddy clothes and torn sleeves. "You look like you tangled with the mountain."

"Mountain won," Tyler muttered.

The busboy laughed softly.

He looked back toward the lodge again. "What is this place?"

"Walnut Lodge," the young man answered proudly, as if the name alone explained everything.

He frowned. "No," he said. "I mean... when did they build this?"

"About three years ago."

He sharply turned toward him. "That's impossible."

The boy blinked. "Sir?"

"I was up here last year. There wasn't anything here."

The busboy only offered a polite smile, though confusion flickered briefly across his face."Well, it's definitely been here longer than that. Busy season too. Especially tonight."

"What's tonight?"

"Masquerade gala." The boy motioned toward the crowd gathering beneath the lights. "Biggest event of the year."

He stared again at the endless stream of arriving guests. Crystal glasses flashed beneath the lantern glow. Laughter echoed warmly across the gravel drive. Somewhere deeper inside the lodge, music swelled louder before fading again. It felt less like East Tennessee and more like he'd stumbled into another time entirely.

The thought should've been ridiculous. Instead it made his skin crawl.

He rubbed a hand across his bruised ribs and looked back toward the dark tree line behind him. The idea of limping all the way back down the mountain suddenly felt unbearable. His cabin sat another several miles away through winding roads and isolated trails. Even if he made it back tonight, he'd spend the evening alone inside a damp little rental box replaying thoughts of Leigh until dawn.

The lodge glowed behind him like a furnace against winter. Warmth. Food. A bed. Maybe answers. He looked down at himself. Mud streaked his jeans nearly black. Blood crusted across his hands and shins. One sleeve hung half torn from his jacket. Definitely not gala material.

"How much are rooms?" he asked reluctantly.

The busboy hesitated just long enough for him to prepare to hear some absurd luxury price. Then the young man leaned slightly closer. "Well… normally around a hundred a night."

Tyler snorted tiredly. "Normally."

"But," the boy continued, lowering his voice, "I've seen hikers come through worse shape than you. Ask the front desk for a room for Marty."

"Marty?"

"That's me." He smiled again. "Tell the front desk I sent you."

He glanced toward the entrance. "What kind of room are we talking about?"

"Staff quarters mostly. Back wing." Marty shrugged. "Same beds. Same heat. Same hot water. Just less fancy wallpaper."

"And the price?"

"Ninety percent discount."

He blinked. "You serious?"

"Ten bucks or so." Marty grinned wider. "Figure the mountain already charged you enough tonight."

For the first time since the fall, he laughed. It hurt. But it felt good anyway.

"That'd save my life," he admitted.

"Maybe the mountain sent you here on purpose."

The words landed strangely. Before he could respond, Marty gave him a quick nod and hurried toward the front entrance, disappearing into the crowd beneath the towering arches. He followed more slowly.

The closer he came to the lodge, the more oppressive its size became. Massive carved doors towered overhead beneath vaulted stonework blackened by age and weather. Iron lanterns hissed softly in the cold wind. Warm air rolled outward from inside carrying scents of cedarwood, smoke, pine resin, and something faintly sweet beneath it all.

Not perfume exactly. Something older. The moment he crossed the threshold, the temperature wrapped around him like a blanket. He stopped dead. The interior was breathtaking. It didn't feel like it was three years old. Maybe 300. Not something just thrown together in the Appalachians, but something that had withstood time. The elements.

Gleaming mahogany stretched across the lobby walls beneath carved arches and towering beams darkened by age. A colossal chandelier of alabaster and brass hung overhead, casting soft amber light across polished marble floors. Oil lamps flickered inside elaborate wall sconces. Thick rugs muted every footstep.

And there were no electronics anywhere. No televisions. No computers. No ringing phones. Not even visible wiring. The entire place felt preserved inside amber.

"Excuse me," he said as he approached the front desk. "I need a room. Marty sent me."

The man behind the desk looked up slowly. Middle-aged perhaps. Maybe older. His dark hair gleamed slick against his scalp, combed so perfectly it appeared painted in place. His charcoal suit looked immaculate, every fold razor sharp.

But it was the eyes that caught Tyler. Black. Not dark brown. Not hazel. Black as wet coal.

"Of course," the clerk said pleasantly. "Marty is one of our finest employees." His voice carried an odd smoothness to it, almost rehearsed. A leather-bound registry slid silently across the counter toward him. He signed without thinking much about it, though the paper itself felt unusually thick beneath his fingers. Heavy. Expensive.

Behind the desk stretched an enormous wall of brass keys organized across 5 ascending rows. Every slot stood full except one. The clerk turned and removed it carefully.

"Busy night?" Tyler asked.

"An important one."

The answer came too quickly. He reached for his wallet, but the clerk gently placed one pale hand over it. The touch startled him. The man's skin felt ice cold.

"That won't be necessary," the clerk said softly. "Marty's guests are always welcome." Something about the statement tightened the back of his neck. Still, exhaustion won out over caution.

"Appreciate it," he muttered.

The clerk handed him the brass key attached to a polished wooden tag. No number. Just a symbol carved into the wood. A crescent moon surrounded by thorn-like markings. Tyler frowned slightly before pocketing it. The deeper he moved into the lodge, the stranger the place became.

Mounted animal heads lined the first hallway beneath cathedral arches. Deer. Elk. Bobcats. Black bears. Even a mountain lion snarling eternally from behind yellowed fangs. Their glass eyes reflected dimly beneath the chandelier light.

One bobcat seemed to follow him as he passed. He looked away quickly. The next corridor displayed framed photographs instead. Old ones. Very old.

Black-and-white portraits stretched along the walls in elaborate gilded frames. Beneath each sat elegant signatures and dates written in fading ink. Charlie Chaplin. Pola Negri. Rudolph Valentino. Douglas Fairbanks. Theda Bara.

He slowed. The photographs looked authentic. Not reproductions. Real. The autographs likewise looked unsettlingly authentic. A strange unease crept steadily through him now. The entire lodge carried the feeling of something disconnected from ordinary time, like a memory that refused to decay properly.

Then he stopped completely. A large framed photograph hung alone beneath a brass light. The plaque beneath it read:

MICHAEL MCKINNEY — GUEST OF THE MONTH

The name hit him with sudden familiarity. Not personal familiarity. Recognition. Like a headline glimpsed years ago. A face attached to some terrible news story he almost remembered but couldn't fully grasp.

Before he could place it, the thought slipped away. His room waited at the far end of the back wing. Even the staff corridor looked lavish compared to most hotels he'd stayed in. Dark floral wallpaper covered the walls beneath carved wooden trim. Velvet sconces glowed softly every few yards. Thick carpet muffled all sound.

The silence bothered him most of all. Despite the crowd in the grand ballroom, the hallway felt dead quiet. He unlocked the room and stepped inside. The door clicked shut behind him with a heavy finality.

He dropped his backpack immediately and let out a long exhausted breath. Pain flared across his body all at once now that he'd stopped moving. His ankle throbbed viciously. Bruises darkened beneath his torn clothes. His shoulder burned where stone had ripped through fabric and skin.

But the room itself felt heavenly. Warm. Still. Safe. A massive bed sat against one wall beneath heavy crimson curtains. Dark wooden furniture gleamed softly beneath lamplight. A small fire crackled inside a stone hearth opposite the bed. For the first time since the fall, he felt something close to relief. The cabin could wait. Leigh could wait. Everything could wait.

He peeled off his torn jacket. He stripped out of the rest of his muddy hiking clothes and stepped into the bathroom. Even that looked impossibly old, but gorgeous nonetheless. Brass fixtures gleamed beneath soft golden light. The shower itself resembled something salvaged from an ocean liner, wide and circular with exposed antique piping climbing the tiled wall.

He turned the handles experimentally. Hot water thundered down over him moments later. The heat struck his bruises like fire at first. Fresh cuts stung sharply beneath the spray. Dirt and dried blood spiraled into the drain around his feet.

But slowly, the tension began easing from his body. His shoulders loosened. The ache in his ribs dulled. Steam filled the room in warm drifting clouds. Water hammered against his skin hard enough to wash away the cold mountain air that clung to him.

He closed his eyes and leaned against the tile. For the first time all day, his mind finally began to quiet. Then, faintly beneath the sound of the water, he heard something else. A voice. It whispered just outside the bathroom door.

Chapter 3

The room should've felt comforting after the fall. Warm. Private. Safe. Instead, he couldn't shake the sensation that something inside the lodge had quietly noticed him the moment he crossed the threshold downstairs.

He lay atop the enormous bed in the dim firelight, wrapped in the thick burgundy robe he'd found hanging inside the armoire, listening to the oppressive stillness pressing against the walls. Exhaustion dragged at every muscle in his body, yet sleep refused to come.

The silence bothered him most. Not ordinary nighttime silence, but something deeper and stranger. There was no wind scratching against the windows, no distant voices echoing through the halls, no creaking pipes hidden in the walls. The lodge felt sealed off from the rest of the world, suspended somewhere outside ordinary life. Only a single sound broke the stillness, the steady ticking of the antique clock mounted beside the fireplace. Tyler stared at the ceiling for several long moments before realizing the rhythm sounded wrong.

He sat upright slowly, but his ribs still ached. He turned toward the clock. The brass carriage-style timepiece gleamed softly in the firelight behind curved glass, its Roman numerals casting warped shadows across the wall. The numbers seemed to morph in the corner of his eye, but returned to normal when he looked directly at them.

The second hand moved steadily counterclockwise. He frowned, thinking at first the mechanism must've been broken, but then the minute hand shifted backward too. A cold sensation crawled beneath the warmth of the robe and settled across his shoulders.

He crossed the room and studied the clock more closely, listening to the backward ticking echo faintly through the suite. Maybe it was some bizarre decorative piece, something meant to unsettle guests during the masquerade downstairs.

Wealthy people loved strange gimmicks, especially in places trying too hard to appear mysterious. Still, the sight of the hands turning in reverse made his stomach tighten unpleasantly. The lodge already felt disconnected from reality, and the clock only deepened the feeling.

He moved toward the tall window and pulled the heavy curtain aside. He needed some air. Below, the gravel drive remained crowded with guests drifting beneath pools of lantern light. A woman in a silver flapper dress laughed while smoke curled from a long cigarette holder between her fingers.

Nearby, a man in a white tailcoat leaned against an antique automobile, calmly smoking a pipe beneath the glow of a gas lamp. Nobody carried phones. Nobody wore anything remotely modern beneath the elegant costumes.

The longer he watched them, the stranger they appeared. These people didn't move like tourists attending a themed party or actors playing dress-up for the evening. Their clothing looked worn naturally, their mannerisms effortless, their conversations genuine rather than performative.

Even the cars and carriages seemed too authentic, polished with the kind of care reserved for objects still regularly used. He felt the uneasy realization creeping deeper into his thoughts. It no longer felt like he had stumbled into a masquerade. It felt like he'd stumbled into another era entirely.

He let the curtain fall shut and stood quietly in the center of the room. Fatigue had faded beneath growing curiosity, sharp enough now that he couldn't ignore it. Nothing about the lodge made sense. Three years old? Impossible. A hidden luxury hotel buried inside protected mountain land without rumors, permits, or internet presence? The whole thing felt concealed in a way that went beyond secrecy. It felt deliberately hidden.

Tyler pulled a fresh pair of pants on. He winced as denim scraped against cuts on his legs and knees. He shoved his feet into his boots, tied them loosely. He slipped the heavy brass key into the robe pocket before opening the door.

The hallway outside stood empty beneath rows of glowing amber sconces. Framed paintings lined the walls between dark stretches of wallpaper patterned with faded vines and flowers. The landscapes looked normal at first glance, but the longer he stared at them, the more distorted they seemed.

One painting showed a mountain ridge beneath a bruised black sky. The trees along its slopes bent into shapes almost resembling human hands. Another depicted a river valley swallowed in unnatural fog, where vague figures appeared hidden among the woods. He quickly looked away and continued down the corridor, disturbed by how alive the artwork felt in the dim light. The deeper he moved into the staff wing, the quieter the lodge became. The silence no longer felt peaceful. It felt deliberate.

He passed a narrow door marked LINEN STORAGE, then another labeled BOILER ACCESS — AUTHORIZED PERSONNEL ONLY. He tried the handle out of instinct. He hoped he'd finally find something normal behind one of these doors. Pipes. Furnaces. Electrical wiring. Anything proving the lodge belonged in the modern world. That this was all just part of the masquerade. The handle refused to budge. He continued farther down the hall until he noticed another door standing partially open near the end of the corridor.

There was no label this time. Only darkness beyond the narrow opening. He glanced back over his shoulder, half expecting to find someone watching him from the hall, but the corridor remained empty.

He slowly nudged the door wider. A narrow staircase descended into darkness below, illuminated only by a single exposed bulb hanging from a frayed cord overhead. The bulb swayed gently back and forth.

He frowned. There wasn't any breeze, yet the light rocked slowly above the stairwell. It threw long shifting shadows across the walls. Somewhere below, a faint creak echoed upward through the darkness. He hesitated for several seconds before finally starting down the stairs, one careful step at a time. The air grew colder with every level he descended.

By the time he reached the bottom, the warmth of the upper floors had vanished completely. The basement corridor smelled damp and ancient. The scent of mildew mixing with rust and wet stone. Exposed pipes snaked along the low ceiling like veins disappearing into shadow. The luxury of the lodge disappeared down here. Bare concrete walls and industrial fixtures replaced polished wood and velvet wallpaper.

To his left stood a thick institutional-looking metal door painted gray. To his right, another staircase continued downward beneath the foundation into deeper darkness. He stared toward the lower stairwell for a long moment, unsettled by the faint draft drifting upward from below. The air smelled earthy down there, almost grave-like. He finally turned away and reached for the metal door instead.

The hinges groaned loudly as he pushed it open. Inside sat a cramped maintenance office lit by a single desk lamp with a yellowed shade. Filing cabinets lined the concrete walls, and dust blanketed nearly every surface. Tyler stepped carefully inside, scanning stacks of papers spread across the desk. Most looked mundane at first glance, maintenance reports and staff records arranged in neat piles.

Then he noticed the dates. Every form looked old. Not artificially aged or yellowed for effect, but genuinely old. Tyler flipped through another stack and found more dates from the late 1920s written in fading ink. A strange pressure settled into his chest as he moved deeper into the office. On the far wall hung a crooked calendar displaying December 1928.

A thick red X marked the fifteenth day. Scrawled across the top in elegant fountain-pen ink was a familiar name. MICHAEL MCKINNEY.

He froze and stared at it. Recognition flickered again somewhere deep in his memory, stronger now than before. The name felt connected to something terrible, something buried in an old headline or half-forgotten story. Before he could fully grasp it, the thought slipped away once more and dissolved into frustration.

Beside the desk sat a metal trash bin filled with blackened ash and burned paper. Resting on top was a partially burned guest registry. Tyler lifted it carefully and opened the brittle pages. Elegant handwriting filled each line beside room numbers and arrival dates. Most guests had departure dates listed beside their names. One did not.

MCKINNEY, M.
Checked in: Oct. 2, 1928
Checked out: —

Blank. He stared at the unfinished entry while a cold heaviness settled over the room. Somewhere above him, the pipes groaned softly inside the walls, the sound strangely human in the silence. Then another noise echoed faintly through the hallway outside. A metallic clank. He slowly closed the registry and looked toward the office door. The basement no longer felt abandoned.

He crossed the room quietly and eased the door shut behind him. The corridor outside remained empty, but the atmosphere had changed completely. Someone else was down there now.

He couldn't explain how he knew it, only that the feeling settled heavily into his gut the moment he stepped back into the hall. He couldn't see or hear another person, but he felt someone. He headed for the stairs immediately, climbing faster with each passing second.

By the time he reached the upper floors again, his pulse hammered against his bruised ribs. He didn't return to his room. Instead, he headed straight toward the main lobby, needing answers before his imagination completely ran away from him. The corridors seemed longer now, dimmer, the paintings watching him from their frames as he passed beneath the flickering sconces.

When he stepped into the lobby, he stopped cold. The massive room stood completely deserted. The chandelier still glowed warmly overhead while fire crackled inside the enormous stone hearth. Cigarette smoke still lingered faintly in the air, as though the crowd had vanished only moments earlier, yet every guest, every servant, every trace of life had disappeared with them.

He slowly turned toward the front desk. Behind it, the wall of brass room keys gleamed beneath the chandelier light. Earlier, only one slot had stood empty. Now there were two. One belonged to his room. The other sat several rows higher, unlabeled and dark, waiting like something reserved long before his arrival.

A soft click echoed somewhere behind him. He froze as a door opened deeper inside the lodge. A slow footstep followed, then another, deliberate and measured against the polished floorboards. The sound drifted steadily closer through the empty halls while he backed away from the desk, suddenly aware of how loud his breathing sounded in the silence.

Were the people returning? Had they only stepped outside for a moment? He glanced down at his clothes and realized immediately he would not fit among them. He returned to his room. The lodge no longer felt luxurious. It felt awake.

Chapter 4

He changed into the cleanest clothes buried inside his backpack, a pair of wrinkled khaki pants and a navy flannel shirt that still smelled faintly of campfire smoke and cedar. Hardly formal wear, but compared to the blood-streaked hiking clothes crumpled on the bathroom floor, it felt respectable enough.

He needed to find out where everyone went. It should be much too early for a party like that to end. Maybe he could pass himself off as some rugged outdoorsman or eccentric traveler who wandered in late from the wilderness. If anyone questioned him, he'd laugh it off and blame the mountain. After everything that had happened since sunset, the explanation almost sounded believable.

When he stepped back into the hallway, the lodge had changed again. Earlier, the corridors had felt watchful and suffocating, every shadow carrying the impression of hidden movement just beyond sight. Now the atmosphere felt strangely subdued, almost sleepy. Sconces burned lower along the walls, their amber light pooling softly across the wallpaper and dark carpeting, while distant music drifted faintly through the building like sound traveling underwater. He paused outside his room for a moment, listening to the muffled orchestra somewhere deeper inside the lodge. Finally. There was sound.

The music pulled at him despite himself. He followed it through the corridors, toward the main foyer, where the towering chandeliers glowed dimly above the empty front desk. The clerk was gone again. No staff moved through the lobby. No guests lingered near the hearth. Yet the lodge no longer felt abandoned. The music breathing through the walls gave the entire place a pulse now, steady and alive, while faint laughter echoed somewhere far beyond the marble archways.

Ahead of him stood a pair of enormous ballroom doors carved from dark polished wood. He had barely started toward them when one of the doors creaked inward on its own. A tall man in a black tuxedo stood waiting in the narrow opening, pale hands folded neatly behind his back. His face looked unnaturally smooth beneath the warm light, almost waxy, while dark half-moons hung beneath his eyes like bruises. He smiled politely, though the expression never quite reached those strange hollow eyes. "How do you do, sir?" His voice was soft as velvet.

Something about him reminded Tyler immediately of Marty, though the resemblance sat somewhere deeper than appearance. The same careful politeness. The same oddly rehearsed warmth. But this man stood too still, too perfectly composed, like an actor frozen in place between scenes. He hesitated for only a second before nodding politely and stepping through the doorway into the ballroom.

The sight beyond it stopped him cold. The room stretched outward on a scale that felt impossible for a structure hidden atop a mountain. Massive vaulted ceilings arched overhead, painted with sprawling frescoes of clouds, angels, twilight skies, and distant stars fading into darkness. Eight enormous marble columns rose from the ballroom floor like the trunks of ancient trees, their polished surfaces gleaming beneath colossal chandeliers. The sheer size of the place made him feel suddenly small, swallowed whole by a world that shouldn't have existed anywhere near Roan Mountain.

The masquerade itself unfolded in full force around him. A live orchestra played beneath a crimson velvet canopy near the far wall, brass instruments gleaming beneath the chandelier light while upright basses and violins carried the melody across the crowded floor.

He recognized the tune almost immediately. "Hello, My Baby." Hearing it performed live, by an honest-to-God big band, triggered a sudden memory of old cartoons from childhood. For one surreal moment, he half expected Daffy Duck to come waddling across the dance floor. Instead, elegantly dressed guests drifted in graceful circles beneath the music, their laughter blending into the rise and fall of the orchestra.

The costumes looked less like party attire and more like genuine clothing from another era. Women wore sequined flapper dresses in deep emeralds, golds, and violets that shimmered every time they moved. Men drifted through the crowd in tuxedos, military coats, silk capes, and tailored suits complete with pocket watches and polished shoes.

A man dressed as a vampire laughed loudly beside a woman wearing a feathered Mardi Gras mask while another couple crossed the floor in powdered wigs straight out of the eighteenth century. Yet despite his plain clothes and obvious lack of refinement, nobody gave him a second glance.

That suited him perfectly. He slipped quietly into the flow of the ballroom, weaving through conversations and dancers while trying not to stand out. After the disaster on the mountain and the strange discoveries downstairs, he found himself oddly grateful simply to be surrounded by people again, even strange ones.

The warmth of the ballroom pressed pleasantly against his skin while laughter and music filled spaces the lodge's silence had left unsettled earlier. For the first time since the fall, some of the tension inside him finally began to loosen.

"Hello." The voice came softly from behind him.

Tyler turned and found a woman standing beside one of the marble columns. She wore a flowing black dress trimmed with silver embroidery, along with a white Venetian mask that covered the upper half of her face. Dark bobbed hair framed pale skin and sharply painted lips. Her posture carried a quiet confidence that immediately drew his attention. Something about her stirred recognition in the back of his mind before he realized what it was.

She looked remarkably like Theda Bara. Not just vaguely similar. Nearly identical to photographs he'd seen years ago from silent film magazines and old documentaries. Even the costume resembled something from *A Fool There Was*, dark and dramatic in that unmistakable early Hollywood style.

Eventually another man in a tuxedo approached her from the crowd. Tyler used the interruption as an excuse to drift away politely. He moved deeper into the ballroom, passing clusters of laughing guests beneath waves of golden light and cigarette smoke.

A blonde woman in pearls flashed him a playful smile while gliding past with a champagne glass in hand, but he only nodded politely and continued on. Everywhere he looked, color and movement dazzled beneath the chandeliers. The wealth surrounding him bordered on absurd.

He had been to costume parties before, mostly cheap college Halloween gatherings with plastic masks and fake cobwebs hanging from apartment ceilings. This was something entirely different. The fabrics looked authentic. Velvet coats draped naturally across shoulders. Sequins and gemstones caught the light with the unmistakable glimmer of the real thing. Even the masks appeared handcrafted rather than mass-produced, delicate and intricate beneath the ballroom lights.

The deeper he moved into the crowd, the more the entire lodge began feeling detached from ordinary reality. Not staged exactly. Preserved. Like a memory refusing to die.

Eventually he reached the long mahogany bar stretching along one side of the ballroom. Behind it stood a sharply dressed bartender in a white dinner jacket with polished silver buttons gleaming beneath the chandeliers. The man's posture looked military straight, his expression calm and professional in a way that reminded Tyler of photographs from old luxury hotels and ocean liners.

"What'll you have, sir?" the bartender asked smoothly.

Tyler opened his mouth automatically. "Uh… beer?"

The bartender blinked once. Not offended exactly, but visibly caught off guard. He suddenly felt like somebody requesting sweet tea at Buckingham Palace. "Actually," he corrected quickly, "make that champagne."

The bartender's polite smile returned immediately. "Of course, sir." He lifted a frosted bottle from an ice bucket and poured pale gold liquid into a crystal flute with practiced elegance. Tyler reached instinctively for his wallet, but the bartender raised one gloved hand before he could pull it free.

"No need, sir."

He frowned. "You sure? I can at least leave a tip."

"The Lodge provides gratuity," the bartender replied pleasantly. "But the gesture is appreciated."

He hesitated another moment before finally nodding. "Well… thanks." The champagne was dry and sharp against his tongue. Cool bubbles fizzing pleasantly after the stale mountain air and lingering taste of blood from earlier. He took another sip while leaning against the polished bar, letting himself relax for the first time all evening.

Across the ballroom, a heavyset man erupted into thunderous laughter while leaning against one of the marble columns. Tears nearly streamed down his face as several others around him joined in. The laughter spread naturally through the room. He found himself smiling despite everything.

Maybe everyone here's just drunk, he thought. *Maybe that's all this is.* Oddly enough, the explanation comforted him.

He drifted away from the bar with the champagne glass still in hand. He moved deeper into the current of music and conversation while the ballroom swirled around him in gold and crimson light. The memory of the cliff faintly lingered in his muscles, along with the unsettling discoveries hidden beneath the lodge. But here, inside the ballroom's warmth and glamour, those fears felt temporarily distant. The Walnut Lodge no longer seemed silent or abandoned.

Here it breathed. Alive with music. Drenched in color. Entirely untouched by time. And somewhere beneath the laughter and orchestra music, he couldn't shake the feeling that something unseen watched him from behind the masks.

Chapter 5

He eventually drifted away from the center of the ballroom, champagne glass still in hand, needing distance from the heat and constant movement. The music had begun settling into his skull, brass and piano notes folding endlessly into laughter and clinking crystal until the entire room felt dreamlike.

He slipped through a side corridor lined with tall windows. He stepped onto the veranda that overlooked the dark mountainside beyond the lodge. The moment the doors closed behind him, the noise softened dramatically, reduced to a dull golden hum trapped behind thick walls and velvet curtains. Cool mountain air washed across his face. For the first time in nearly an hour, he could breathe clearly again.

The veranda stretched the length of the ballroom, broad and elegant beneath hanging lanterns that cast warm pools of amber light across polished stone. Beyond the balustrade, the mountains disappeared into endless black ridges. They layered against the horizon beneath a pale wash of moonlight. Pine trees whispered somewhere below the cliffs, while cold wind carried the scent of damp stone, chimney smoke, and approaching rain. Compared to the overwhelming glamour inside, the quiet outside felt almost sacred. But he wasn't alone out there.

A small group of guests stood gathered near the far end of the veranda in a loose crescent beneath one of the lanterns. Half a dozen people, maybe more. Unlike the revelers inside, none of them danced or laughed or carried drinks. They stood quietly together in stiff little clusters, hands folded neatly in front of them or resting at their sides. The atmosphere around them reminded Tyler uncomfortably of mourners waiting outside a funeral chapel after the service had ended.

As he wandered closer, one of the men detached himself from the group and approached with measured, deliberate steps. He was tall and painfully thin, dressed in a perfectly tailored tuxedo with a black silk top hat tilted at an exact angle atop neatly combed silver hair. His smile looked strained somehow, stretched tightly across his face like a drawstring pulled too hard.

"Good evening," the man said smoothly, extending one white-gloved hand. "Charles Worthington… the Third."

Tyler shook it politely. "Tyler," he said.

"A pleasure," Charles replied, though his tone suggested the opposite.

The handshake lasted barely a second. Charles released him immediately afterward with the strange care of someone touching something unclean. He half expected the man to reach for a handkerchief and discreetly wipe his glove clean afterward.

Another figure stepped gracefully from the group before the silence could settle too heavily between them. A woman in a dark emerald flapper dress approached with careful elegance, every green sequin perfectly arranged beneath the lantern light. A glittering silver mask concealed the upper half of her face, though her eyes remained unreadable behind it.

"Hello," she said sweetly. "I'm Sarah Cook."

Tyler nodded politely. "Nice to meet you."

Her smile lingered a little too long. Before either could continue, another man appeared from behind the others, tall and narrow-shouldered with hollow eyes and a neatly trimmed mustache. Dark hair gleamed beneath the veranda lanterns, slicked tightly to one side in an old-fashioned style that immediately reminded Tyler of antique portraits.

The man looked disturbingly like Edgar Allan Poe dressed for a society gala. "My name is Frank Stein," he said solemnly.

Tyler blinked once. "Like Frankenstein?"

Frank smiled faintly, though no warmth reached his eyes. "Exactly like Frankenstein."

The answer hung awkwardly in the cold night air. Tyler opened his mouth to respond, but another hand suddenly extended toward him from the edge of the group. This time the face attached to it made his stomach tighten immediately.

"Michael McKinney," the man said calmly.

Tyler hesitated. Only briefly. But long enough for the pause to become noticeable. Still, he shook the offered hand. Michael looked completely alive. Mid-thirties maybe. Sharp jawline. Healthy complexion. Dark suit pressed perfectly against broad shoulders. Nothing ghostly or corpse-like about him whatsoever. Yet Tyler recognized the name instantly now. The registry downstairs. The unfinished check-out date. The photograph hanging in the hall.

Michael McKinney. "You enjoying the Lodge?" Michael asked pleasantly.

Tyler studied him carefully. "I think so."

"That's good."

The answer came automatically, almost mechanically.

"You've been here long?" Tyler asked.

A strange expression flickered across Michael's face for the briefest moment. Not sadness exactly. Weariness perhaps. "A while," he said quietly.

Nothing more. No elaboration. No explanation. Just that same faint smile that never fully reached his eyes.

He felt the unease creeping back into him immediately. He glanced toward the ballroom doors behind him where muffled music still drifted faintly through the walls. The people gathered out here felt disconnected from the celebration inside. They weren't part of its rhythm. They stood apart from it entirely, as though they belonged to another gathering the rest of the guests couldn't see.

Charles stepped forward again, interrupting the silence before it grew uncomfortable. "Tyler, my lad," he said smoothly. "Care to join us for a brandy?"

Something about the invitation unsettled him instantly. Charles smiled too carefully while offering it, like a spider politely inviting a fly to sit closer to the web.

Tyler forced a casual grin. "Maybe in a bit. I'm still exploring the place."

"Of course," Charles replied. The smile tightened slightly.

Oddly enough, Tyler thought he detected relief hidden beneath it. As though Charles didn't truly want him staying there either.

"Well," Tyler said lightly, stepping backward toward the ballroom doors, "I'll see you folks around."

"Without question," Frank Stein murmured.

The way he said it made Tyler's skin prickle. He slipped back inside without saying another word. Warmth and music swallowed him immediately as the ballroom surged around him once more in waves of color and sound.

The orchestra had shifted songs, though the new tune sounded strangely similar to the last, carrying the same looping, hypnotic rhythm through the crowd. Couples still danced beneath the chandeliers. Laughter still echoed between the marble columns. Champagne still flowed endlessly from silver trays drifting through the room.

Yet something felt subtly wrong now. The ballroom no longer seemed lively so much as repetitive. He slowed near the edge of the dance floor and quietly studied the crowd. The same blonde woman in pearls crossed the room again. The same heavyset man laughed thunderously beside the same column. The same vampire-costumed guest spun the same woman beneath the chandeliers.

It felt less like a party continuing naturally and more like a scene repeating itself endlessly just beneath the threshold of notice. Time inside the Walnut Lodge had begun feeling sticky. Unmoving. Like the night itself refused to advance beyond a certain hour.

He took another sip of champagne, though his stomach rolled uneasily afterward. Earlier he'd blamed the nausea on the fall and adrenaline, but now he wasn't so sure. Something deeper unsettled him. Something buried beneath the music and glamour, like rot beneath polished floorboards.

A waiter drifted past carrying silver trays loaded with tiny canapés topped with cream and black fish eggs. Tyler had tried one earlier out of politeness and nearly gagged the moment it touched his tongue. The texture alone turned his stomach. Even now, the scent rising from the trays made nausea tighten sharply in his throat.

Nobody else seemed bothered. The guests drank endlessly without slurring their speech or stumbling. They danced without exhaustion. Waiters carried away empty trays only for full ones to appear moments later. Nobody argued. Nobody grew tired. Nobody looked ready to leave.

And suddenly he realized something that made the back of his neck go cold. He hadn't seen a single person leave the ballroom all evening. Not one.

People drifted into adjoining lounges and side halls before eventually returning again, but no one collected coats. No one said goodbye. No carriages departed outside the windows. The celebration simply continued in smooth endless circles beneath the chandeliers.

More champagne. More dancing. More laughter. A party trapped somewhere outside ordinary time. He looked back toward the veranda doors. The group outside remained visible only as silhouettes now beneath the lantern glow. Silent. Motionless. Watching through the glass.

He took another slow sip from the champagne flute while unease settled deeper into his chest. Then, for the first time since entering the lodge, a thought occurred to him that he couldn't shake away. Maybe walking through those front doors had been a mistake after all.

Chapter 6

The champagne slowly lost its chill in his hand. He stood near the edge of the ballroom beneath the shadow of one of the towering marble columns, absently turning the crystal stem between his fingers while the orchestra thundered on without pause.

The same looping rhythm filled the enormous room again and again, brass swelling beneath strings while dancers drifted endlessly beneath the chandeliers. No one appeared tired. No one stumbled away for air or slipped off toward bed. The celebration simply continued in smooth, polished circles like a clock whose hands had stopped moving while the gears underneath kept turning forever.

He scanned the crowd carefully now. The same faces kept resurfacing. The blonde woman with the pearl necklace drifted past him again carrying another untouched flute of champagne. The vampire-costumed man still danced with the same masked woman beneath the lights. The heavyset guest near the orchestra erupted into another roaring laugh that sounded nearly identical to the one Tyler had heard ten minutes earlier.

It wasn't just repetition. It felt rehearsed. His stomach tightened uneasily. And then another thought occurred to him. No one had checked their phone all night, either. Not one glowing screen. Not one ringing notification. Nobody texting. Nobody taking pictures. Nobody leaning into a corner pretending to care about a conversation while secretly scrolling through social media beneath the table.

Do they even have phones? The question settled strangely in his mind.

He looked down at the champagne in his hand and realized he no longer wanted it. The bubbles had faded. The drink sat untouched now except for a few cautious sips. He crossed toward a small table near one of the columns and set the glass down carefully beside an elaborate bronze ashtray before slipping away from the heart of the ballroom.

Almost immediately, the atmosphere changed. The farther he moved from the orchestra, the more muffled the music became until only the distant pulse of brass and piano echoed faintly through the walls.

He wandered into a quieter side corridor branching away from the ballroom's western wing, one apparently used far less often by the guests. The lighting dimmed noticeably here. Gone were the glittering chandeliers and endless movement. Warm amber sconces cast softer pools of light along dark paneled walls while heavy oil paintings loomed overhead in ornate golden frames.

Tyler slowed his pace. Every portrait seemed to watch him. Severe-looking men in black coats and stiff collars stared outward with expressionless eyes while pale women posed beneath layers of velvet and lace against backgrounds swallowed in shadow. None of the paintings displayed dates or plaques. The farther he walked, the older they seemed to become. One portrait showed a bearded man standing beside an enormous phonograph while another depicted a woman seated near heavy curtains with one hand resting atop a closed casket-sized trunk.

The floor changed beneath Tyler's boots as well. The polished marble gave way to dark hardwood worn smooth with age, partially covered by thick crimson runners that muffled every footstep. The corridor felt warmer than the basement below the lodge, yet somehow less alive than the ballroom behind him. Quiet hung heavily in the air.

He found himself thinking about his room. Maybe he should just go back. Lock the door. Get some sleep. Everything about the Walnut Lodge had grown stranger with every passing hour, and exhaustion still clung stubbornly to his muscles after the fall on the mountain.

Then he felt it. A draft. Cold air brushed softly against the right side of his face. He stopped immediately. The corridor stood completely enclosed. No open windows. No visible doors nearby except the ones he'd already passed. Yet the breeze continued faintly against his skin, subtle but unmistakable.

He frowned and turned slowly toward the wall. The carved wooden paneling looked seamless at first glance, rich dark wood etched with intricate floral patterns and twisting vines polished smooth with age. He stepped closer and ran his fingers lightly across the grooves. The wood felt colder in one section near eye level.

Then he found it. A seam. Barely visible. Just a thin hairline fracture hidden between the carved panels. He pressed gently against it. Nothing happened.

He glanced back down the corridor. Still empty. Still silent except for the distant pulse of orchestra music somewhere far behind him. Carefully, he leaned one shoulder against the panel and pushed harder. Wood creaked softly. The hidden section swung inward. Darkness waited beyond it.

Not a room exactly. More like a narrow passage carved directly into the bones of the lodge itself. He hesitated. Every instinct told him to walk away. Instead, he slipped inside. The panel clicked shut behind him with a sound soft enough to raise the hairs on the back of his neck.

The hidden corridor was impossibly narrow, forcing him to hunch slightly beneath the low ceiling. Rough unfinished wood lined the walls here, old timber stripped bare of the lodge's polished elegance. Dust coated nearly every surface. The air smelled stale and cold, carrying traces of mildew and something else beneath it.

Something medicinal. Or rotten.

He reached instinctively into his pocket and pulled out his phone. The screen flickered once. Then died. Black. "No," he muttered under his breath, pressing the button again. Nothing. Dead. Of course it was.

He slipped it back into his pocket and continued forward carefully, one hand trailing along the rough wall for balance. The darkness pressed tightly around him now. Somewhere overhead, the lodge groaned softly inside its ancient framework. The further he moved, the more the hidden passage reminded him of old coal tunnels he'd explored as a teenager back in abandoned mining country.

Claustrophobic. Airless. Wrong. Then, after several careful steps, he saw light ahead. A faint sliver of yellow glowed beneath another wooden panel farther down the passage. He slowed immediately.

Voices drifted faintly through the crack. At first he couldn't make out the words. Just soft conversation somewhere beyond the wall. No music. No laughter. Nothing like the ballroom outside. This sounded private. Careful. He moved closer until he could hear clearly.

"…he's not one of them," a man said quietly.

The voice sounded calm and educated, each word measured with precise control.

"No," a woman replied. "But he's seen too much already. The fall wasn't enough."

He felt something inside his stomach twist hard. He stood completely motionless now, scarcely breathing.

"I'll speak with Charles," the man continued. "He was careless bringing him here. The boy should've been left at the cliff."

Silence followed briefly. Then the woman spoke again. "Do you think he knows?"

"Not yet," the man answered. "But if he keeps wandering, he'll find it."

He backed away from the wall immediately, pulse hammering violently inside his chest. The casualness of the conversation frightened him more than the words themselves. They weren't whispering in panic or anger. They sounded calm. Practical. As though discussing whether a stranger should've died at the bottom of a ravine was no more important than deciding what wine to serve at dinner.

He turned carefully and started back through the narrow passage, moving as quietly as possible. Suddenly the corridor felt tighter than before. The darkness thicker. Every creak of wood overhead made him flinch. The stale air seemed heavier now too, pressing against his chest while distant sounds from the ballroom faded further and further away.

For one awful moment, Tyler became convinced the hidden corridor didn't want him leaving. The irrational thought settled over him so strongly he nearly stopped moving altogether. He reached the entrance panel at last and shoved hard against it. Nothing.

The wood refused to move. His breathing quickened. "Come on…." He pushed harder. The panel groaned loudly before finally swinging outward. He stumbled back into the hallway so quickly he nearly lost his footing.

The corridor outside looked subtly different now. Dimmer somehow. The electric lights flickered softly with a warm uneven glow more like gas lamps than modern bulbs. Shadows stretched longer across the floor. Even the portraits lining the walls appeared darker, their painted faces more severe than before. One old man's eyes seemed fixed directly on him, now in a way they definitely hadn't been earlier.

He didn't stop walking. He moved quickly down the corridor, past the velvet runners and heavy paintings, trying hard not to look too closely at anything around him. The farther he went, the louder the ballroom music became again until brass and piano finally swallowed the silence completely. When he stepped back into the ballroom, nothing had changed.

The orchestra still played beneath the crimson canopy. The dancers still turned endlessly beneath the chandeliers. The same laughter echoed between the marble columns. No one looked toward him. No one appeared to notice he'd been gone at all.

He spotted his champagne glass exactly where he'd left it near the bronze ashtray. A single bead of condensation rolled slowly down the crystal stem beneath the ballroom lights.

He picked the glass up automatically. Then paused. For several long seconds, he simply stared at the pale gold liquid inside. Finally, he set it back down untouched. And this time, he walked away without taking another sip.

Chapter 7

Tyler woke with a violent jolt, lungs dragging in air before his mind fully understood why. For several disoriented seconds, he simply sat upright in the dark clutching at the blankets while the room slowly settled back into focus around him. Firelight flickered weakly inside the stone hearth across the suite, casting long shadows against the ceiling beams.

The antique clock still ticked softly beside the mantle, though thankfully forward again, at least for now. His body ached everywhere. Bruised ribs protested every breath. His legs felt heavy from the mountain climb and the fall. He should've been exhausted enough to sleep until noon. Instead, every nerve in his body buzzed with restless alertness.

It felt less like waking naturally and more like something had quietly nudged him out of sleep. He rubbed both hands over his face and tried grounding himself. Maybe adrenaline still lingered from the evening. Maybe the bizarre atmosphere of the lodge had simply worked its way too deeply into his head. Either way, genuine rest seemed impossible inside the Walnut Lodge. Even lying in bed, he'd carried the uneasy sensation that the building itself remained awake around him, listening quietly through the walls while he slept.

Then he heard the music. Faint at first. A distant trumpet somewhere overhead. Laughter followed. He lowered his hands slowly and stared toward the ceiling. The party was still going.

Not quieter exactly. Farther away perhaps. Muffled now by floors and walls, yet unmistakably alive somewhere above him. Music drifted through the lodge in slow ghostly pulses while scattered laughter echoed faintly between notes.

He glanced toward the clock. A little after midnight. "That's one hell of a party," he muttered quietly.

Most events would've died hours ago. By midnight, people should've been slumped drunk in chairs or wandering toward elevators with loosened ties and smeared lipstick. Instead the ballroom still sounded energetic. Vibrant. As though the evening had barely begun.

He swung his legs carefully over the side of the bed and stood. His muscles complained immediately. Bruises darkened deeper along his ribs now, and his shoulder remained stiff from slamming against the mountainside earlier. Still, curiosity outweighed exhaustion.

If the party kept going this late, maybe people would finally loosen up. Maybe he'd get real answers. Drunk people talked.

He pulled on his navy flannel shirt again and shoved his feet into his boots before stepping carefully into the hallway outside. The staff wing remained quiet beneath its dim amber sconces, though the silence no longer felt quite as oppressive as earlier. The distant orchestra softened the edges of the lodge's emptiness now, giving the entire building the strange illusion of life pulsing somewhere above.

He headed toward the elevator. The polished brass doors reflected him faintly beneath the hallway lights as he approached. He hesitated before pressing the call button, suddenly remembering the eerie bellboy from earlier and the unnatural stillness he carried everywhere like a shadow sewn into human shape.

Part of him dreaded sharing another ride with him. The elevator rattled somewhere beyond the walls. Chains groaned. Metal clanked softly upward through the shaft. When the doors finally slid open, the elevator stood empty.

He released a breath he hadn't realized he was holding and stepped inside quickly before something changed its mind. The accordion gate folded shut behind him with a metallic scrape. Moments later, the old lift lurched upward hard enough to nearly throw him off balance.

The machinery sounded terrible. Not broken exactly. Ancient. Every passing floor triggered fresh grinding noises inside the shaft while cables strained overhead with long metallic groans. The elevator shook constantly during the ascent, trembling beneath his boots like an exhausted animal forced to keep climbing long after its legs gave out.

By the time the lift shuddered to a stop on the fourth floor, Tyler felt like he'd narrowly survived some elaborate death trap from another century. The doors creaked open. He stepped out slowly. And immediately realized this floor was nothing like the others.

The atmosphere changed the moment he entered the hallway. The lower levels of the lodge had been luxurious, yes, but this felt opulent in a way bordering on royal. Thick velvet carpet cushioned every footstep beneath intricate patterns woven in gold thread. Massive gilded sconces lined the walls, though these held actual candles rather than electric bulbs. Their flames flickered softly beneath painted ceiling murals depicting clouds, angels, and elaborate scenes he couldn't fully make out in the dim light.

The air even smelled different here. Not dust and old wood anymore. Incense. Perfume. Old money. He turned slowly, taking it all in. "My floor definitely didn't look like this."

His room downstairs suddenly felt tiny by comparison. Functional. Plain. This upper level belonged to another class of guest entirely, people who apparently lived inside the highest layers of the lodge's strange hierarchy. The music sounded louder here too. Clearer.

He followed it instinctively through the corridor, deeper into the fourth floor while candlelight flickered softly across the walls. Somewhere ahead, the orchestra surged triumphantly into another song while laughter echoed warmly beyond a pair of towering double doors.

Tyler approached cautiously. Out of habit more than politeness, he knocked once. The doors swung inward on their own. The penthouse ballroom beyond exploded with motion and light. He stopped dead.

Nothing had changed. Not one thing. The same massive chandeliers blazed overhead. The same guests spun endlessly across the dance floor beneath swells of brass and piano. Laughter rolled through the room in rich waves while waiters drifted between guests carrying endless silver trays of champagne.

The orchestra now played a jubilant rendition of "Buffalo Gals," lively and energetic enough to rattle the crystal hanging overhead. But the people… They looked untouched by time. No exhaustion. No drunken collapse. No thinning crowd. No sign the evening had advanced at all since he last stood there. It felt as though the party had simply paused while he slept.

"Tyler!" A voice brightly rang across the dancers near him.

He barely had time to turn before a woman stepped through the crowd toward him. She moved with easy familiarity, as though they already knew one another. He noticed her earlier but didn't know her. Her black dress clung to her like shadow beneath the chandelier light, and a pale Venetian mask concealed part of her face, though her eyes gleamed brightly beneath it.

"There you are," she said softly, almost laughing with relief. "I wondered if you'd come back."

He stared at her, unsettled by the certainty in her voice. He knew they had never met. "Do I know you?"

She tilted her head slightly. "Thea."

"Thea," he repeated.

"Yes." A faint smile touched her lips. "And you're Tyler."

A strange chill passed through him. "How do you know my name?"

Instead of answering, she gave a small turn beneath the chandelier light, the dark fabric of her dress shifting like liquid smoke around her. "Do you like it?"

Tyler blinked. "You look like Theda Bara."

Her smile widened slowly, though something in it felt distant, almost sad. "No one's said that in a very long time."

Then something shifted inside him. Not a memory exactly, but the sudden resurfacing of a vision long buried beneath waking life. A year earlier, during his last hike through the mountains, he had dreamed of a ballroom glowing beneath chandeliers while masked figures drifted endlessly through music he could not quite hear.

He remembered waking unsettled in his cabin while rain tapped softly against the canvas. The dream had faded soon after. And before that, the same thing happened when he last hiked the Roan. She was more familiar to him than his own fiancé, and he wasn't even aware. He didn't remember until he returned to the mountains. Since he arrived in the area, fragments of it had begun creeping back into his mind, piece by piece. Now he stood inside it.

"Come dance with me," she said breathlessly as she reached for his hand. He opened his mouth to protest, but she had already drawn him forward into the current of dancers swirling across the ballroom floor. The movement swallowed him immediately.

Music thundered around them while velvet and silk blurred past in flashes of gold and crimson. Thea danced effortlessly, almost weightless in his arms, guiding him through turns and sweeping steps with unnatural grace. He stumbled at first before muscle memory kicked in.

Leigh. He almost laughed bitterly at the thought. She had insisted on ballroom lessons during one of her "new beginnings" phases a couple years earlier. He'd hated every second of it at the time, but now the steps returned surprisingly easily beneath the music. Foxtrot. Waltz. Even fragments of the Charleston. Thea moved through them all flawlessly.

"You people are insane," Tyler said between breaths after another turn across the floor. "Seriously, what's in the water around here? Nobody's even slowing down."

She laughed and spun beneath his arm. "Why would we slow down?" she asked. "It hasn't been that long."

Something about the phrasing unsettled him immediately. Not the words themselves. The rhythm of them. Like someone imitating ordinary conversation rather than naturally speaking it.

"You dance like this every night?" Tyler asked.

"Oh heavens no," she replied dramatically. "Only when there's reason to celebrate."

"And what are we celebrating?"

She smiled. But once again, the smile stopped just short of reaching her eyes. "You'll see."

The answer sent a faint chill through him despite the warmth of the ballroom. He glanced around the room while they danced. Charles Worthington still stood near one of the marble columns speaking with a cluster of sharply dressed guests. Frank Stein lingered beside the orchestra with the same solemn expression fixed permanently across his face.

Even Michael McKinney remained there beneath the chandeliers, champagne glass in hand, smiling faintly at conversations he doubted he was actually listening to.

Nobody had changed positions much. Nobody looked older. Nobody looked tired. Then suddenly the ballroom erupted into movement. A rush of footsteps thundered across the floor as dozens of guests abruptly turned toward the far doors laughing excitedly.

Women gathered their dresses while men shouted cheerfully over one another. The atmosphere shifted instantly from elegant celebration into something strangely childlike and frantic.

"Oh!" Thea clapped excitedly beside him. "It's time!"

Tyler frowned. "Time for what?"

"The swim."

"The what?"

"The midnight swim, silly." She laughed again and grabbed his hand tightly. "Come on."

He didn't move. "Thea… it's dark outside."

"That's the best part."

Guests nearly bolted out of the ballroom in waves. All of them smiled too widely beneath masks and champagne-flushed faces. The orchestra continued playing while people hurried past laughing like schoolchildren escaping class.

He stared at them uneasily. Their excitement felt genuine. But also rehearsed somehow. Too synchronized. Too perfect.

"We go every night," Thea said eagerly. "You'll love it."

Every night. The phrase landed hard inside his chest. He looked toward the open doors where the crowd disappeared into darkness beyond the lodge. Nobody hesitated. Nobody questioned it. They simply moved together in smooth endless currents while music continued roaring behind them.

Then he looked back at Thea. Her hand still gripped his tightly. Her skin felt warm. Her eyes glittered brightly beneath the mask. But her smile… Her smile looked wrong now. Too wide. Too eager. Too practiced.

He stopped at the edge of the ballroom while the crowd streamed past him toward the night beyond the doors. The dancers moved with perfect rhythm even in their excitement, bodies flowing together like pieces inside some elaborate mechanical performance. And not a single one of them looked back.

Chapter 8

"Okay," Tyler said at last. The crowd surged immediately toward the elevators in a blur of silk, velvet, feathers, and glittering masks. Excited laughter bounced off the marble walls while guests pressed together, eager to reach the midnight swim before anyone else. Thea disappeared briefly into the mass of bodies before turning back toward him again, one pale hand gripping the elevator gate while her white mask sat slightly crooked across her face.

"Come on, Tyler," she called brightly.

He raised a hand apologetically. "I'll take the stairs. That thing already looks overloaded."

"Oh, nonsense," she laughed.

"Thea, seriously. I don't want to get trapped in there with thirty people breathing champagne in my face. I'll beat you downstairs."

She tilted her head slightly. For just a second, disappointment flickered across her expression. "Are you sure you'll come?"

"Positive." The answer came easier than he expected, though something about the question unsettled him. Thea held his gaze another second longer than necessary before finally smiling again. Around her, guests continued packing themselves into the elevator cage shoulder to shoulder while music thundered faintly from the ballroom behind them.

Then Tyler saw him again. The bellboy leaned casually from inside the elevator like a shadow stepping halfway into the world. Pale skin. Perfectly pressed uniform. That same sharp little smile fixed permanently across his face.

"There's room for one more, sir," he said smoothly. Tyler's stomach tightened instantly.

The voice. The smile. It was the exact same bellboy from earlier. Or at least it looked like him. He suddenly couldn't tell anymore whether the man kept reappearing throughout the lodge or had simply never left his post at all. The elevator operator's eyes glittered faintly beneath the overhead lights while he waited patiently for Tyler's answer.

"No," Tyler said carefully. "I'm good."

"You're certain?"

"Pretty sure I'd rather trust stairs than this thing."

The bellboy grinned wider. "Oh, I wouldn't."

Before Tyler could respond, the operator pulled the brass lever beside him with a heavy metallic clack. The accordion gate rattled shut while guests laughed and squeezed together tighter inside the cage. The entire elevator shuddered beneath the weight.

Then it began descending. The machinery groaned horribly. He stood frozen for a moment watching the floor indicator slowly tick downward while the cables above strained loud enough to echo through the shaft.

Why is he still the only one working here? The thought struck him suddenly. The ballroom swarmed with guests. The bar stayed stocked endlessly. Food appeared nonstop from silver trays. Yet aside from the occasional bartender or silent waiter drifting through the crowd, Tyler rarely saw actual staff.

Especially not on the upper floors. And the bellboy... The bellboy always seemed to be there. Watching.

He turned away from the elevator and headed for the staircase instead. The stairwell spiraled elegantly downward through the center of the lodge beneath dim golden sconces. His hand slid along the polished wooden banister as he descended while somewhere nearby the elevator continued grinding lower through the shaft. The sounds it made grew steadily worse.

Metal scraping metal. Cables straining tight overhead. A low rhythmic groaning like something enormous bending under too much pressure.

He slowed near the second-floor landing. The elevator sounded wrong. Not merely old. Dangerous. Another loud metallic creak echoed through the walls.

He stopped completely. The sound came again, deeper this time. A wet twisting groan like steel slowly tearing apart. Then— SNAP.

The noise cracked through the stairwell like a rifle shot. For one impossible second, silence followed. Then the elevator screamed. The entire shaft erupted into violent metallic thunder as the elevator cage plummeted downward at terrifying speed. Guests inside began screaming instantly, raw human panic exploding upward through the stairwell while the cables lashed wildly against the walls.

"Oh God!"

"Stop it!"

"HELP—!"

He ran. He nearly lost his footing flying down the stairs two at a time while the elevator roared beneath him like a missile dropping through the center of the lodge. The sound shook the entire structure. Chandeliers rattled overhead. Dust burst loose from cracks in the ceiling.

Then came the impact. The crash thundered up through the building with enough force to knock him sideways against the railing. He sprinted the remaining steps and burst into the foyer gasping for breath.

The elevator doors downstairs remained closed. Perfectly closed. No blood leaked beneath them. No twisted wreckage burst outward. Nothing. But beneath the polished marble floor, something groaned.

The sound rolled upward through Tyler's boots and into his bones, low and massive like some enormous machine waking beneath the earth. It drowned the screaming briefly before the voices returned louder than before.

"The door won't open!"

"We're trapped!"

Then came Thea's voice. "Tyler!"

Her scream sliced through him. "Tyler, help me!"

He stepped instinctively toward the elevator shaft before stopping himself. The entire wall trembled violently. Another deep roar surged upward from below, powerful enough to shake paintings loose from their hooks. One crashed nearby in an explosion of shattered glass.

He moved closer despite himself and looked down through the fractured opening beside the shaft. The elevator cage sat lodged deep below, bent grotesquely inward like a crushed tin can. Jagged iron bars twisted outward at impossible angles while orange light spilled upward beneath it from somewhere far below the foundation.

Heat rolled from the shaft. A terrified voice echoed upward.

"We hit the boiler!"

"No," another sobbed. "We're on it!"

Then came Charles Worthington's voice, stripped entirely of its smug theatrical elegance. "Oh God," he whimpered. "Why did we put it there?"

He froze. *Put it there?* They knew. Somehow they'd known this would happen. And suddenly understanding hit him with terrifying clarity.

This wasn't an accident. It happened before. Maybe many times before. The elevator groaned again beneath the lodge while flames flickered somewhere below the crushed cage. Guests screamed hysterically now, voices echoing upward from depths He couldn't even fully see. The shaft extended much farther underground than it should have, disappearing into enormous darkness beneath the foundation.

He looked desperately around the foyer. No basement entrance. No emergency release. No way to reach them. Even if there had been, the wreckage below looked unsurvivable. Jagged bars protruded upward through the collapsed elevator roof like iron spears. Steam hissed violently through broken pipes while orange firelight pulsed beneath the cage.

Then Thea screamed again. The sound hit him harder than the others. *Leigh lies to me for months,* he thought wildly. *Vanishes into excuses and fake emergencies and other men.... And then the first woman who actually feels real winds up trapped inside this nightmare.*

For one awful moment he considered jumping. Actually considered it. But the instant he looked down again, he knew it would kill him too. And deeper than logic, something else whispered quietly inside him. *You can't change this.* The thought didn't feel imagined. It felt remembered.

Another violent jolt shook the entire lodge. Cracks splintered across the marble walls. Gas hissed loudly somewhere beneath the floor. The smell hit seconds later, sharp and unmistakable. Natural gas.

"I smell it!" someone shrieked below. "Oh God, I smell gas!"

That snapped him out of it. The place was going to explode. He turned and ran. The foyer stretched strangely long now as he sprinted across the marble floor toward the front entrance. Massive double doors stood wide open ahead of him, cold mountain air flooding inward through swirling curtains of smoke and dust. And standing calmly between the doors waited another bellboy.

He slowed involuntarily. The uniform matched perfectly. The pale face. The smile. Everything. But this wasn't the same one from the elevator. Or maybe it was. He genuinely couldn't tell anymore. The bellboy simply stood there holding the door open politely while chaos erupted behind him.

"Don't you understand?" Tyler shouted as he ran past. "It's going to blow!"

The bellboy didn't even blink. "Certainly, sir," he replied pleasantly. "It does every night."

He stared at him in horror. Behind him, guests continued screaming inside the shaft while the lodge groaned louder and louder around them. The bellboy smiled faintly. "There's still room for one more," he added softly. "Care to join?"

He let out a strangled yell of frustration and bolted past him into the freezing mountain air. They knew. Every single one of them knew. The elevator. The boiler. The gas. This wasn't a tragedy happening for the first time. It was part of the lodge.

Part of whatever terrible ritual or cycle kept the place alive. He hit the top steps at full speed and leapt outward just as the Walnut Lodge exploded behind him.

The blast came with a deafening roar that swallowed the mountain itself. Fire burst outward through the windows in violent orange waves while scorching wind slammed into Tyler midair hard enough to throw him sideways.

He crashed into the hillside shoulder first. The world flipped instantly into chaos. Dirt filled his mouth. Rocks hammered his ribs and legs while momentum carried him tumbling violently down the slope. Branches whipped across his face. His arm struck something hard enough to numb it completely. Sky and earth spun together until he couldn't tell which direction was up anymore.

Then darkness swallowed him whole. Cool. Absolute. And waiting.

Chapter 9

Tyler opened his eyes to birdsong. For several long seconds, he simply lay there blinking against the pale morning light filtering through the trees overhead. Sunlight spilled across the mountainside in soft golden slants while wind stirred gently through pine branches above him. Somewhere nearby, squirrels rustled through dead leaves and brush. The air smelled clean, damp with dew and fresh earth, carrying the rich scent of moss, bark, and cold mountain water.

It was absurdly peaceful. After everything that had happened inside Walnut Lodge, the quiet morning felt unreal in its own way. He almost expected to open his eyes again and find himself back in that enormous ballroom beneath the chandeliers while the orchestra played another endless song.

Instead, the mountain greeted him with birds and sunlight. He lay still a moment longer trying to understand whether he was alive. Pain answered first. Not sharp enough for death. Not distant enough for dreaming.

His entire body ached with the heavy bruised soreness of survival. His ribs burned when he breathed too deeply. His left shoulder throbbed where he'd slammed into the hillside during the explosion. Dirt crusted his hands and jeans. Pine needles clung to his sleeves.

Slowly, he pushed himself upright. The movement sent a violent protest through his spine. His back popped painfully while dizziness swept briefly across his vision. He sat hunched forward catching his breath before finally noticing where he'd landed.

The cliff. Again? He stared in disbelief.

Samson's Cliff loomed only inches behind him, the jagged drop plunging downward through pine shadow exactly as it had the day before. One careless roll in his sleep and he would've fallen straight into the ravine below. He rose carefully to his feet and looked around harder now.

He'd landed maybe forty feet from the exact spot where he first lost his footing yesterday evening. The realization made his stomach tighten. Almost like the mountain had put him back where it found him.

He turned slowly toward the summit above. Dread settled over him immediately. He didn't want to climb back up there. Every instinct screamed against it. The memory of the explosion still rang fresh inside his skull. The screams from the elevator shaft. The heat. The fire. *Thea.*

But he had to know. There would be wreckage at least. Fire crews maybe. Police. Rangers. Something. Dozens of people had died inside that lodge. There had to be evidence left behind.

And if there wasn't… he was likely insane. He didn't know which possibility frightened him more.

He started uphill slowly, muscles protesting every step while morning sunlight filtered through the trees around him. The forest remained perfectly ordinary. Birds hopped through branches overhead. Wind whispered through mountain laurel and pine needles. Somewhere far below, water rushed faintly through unseen creeks.

The normalcy of it all felt wrong now. As though the mountain itself refused to acknowledge what had happened during the night. He finally reached the crest of the hill.

Then stopped dead. The Walnut Lodge was gone. Not burned. Not destroyed. Gone.

The mountaintop stood empty beneath the morning sun, covered in rolling grass and patches of wildflowers swaying gently in the breeze. Trees lined the hill exactly as they should have. Large stones jutted naturally from the earth. Nothing looked scorched. Nothing looked disturbed.

There wasn't even rubble. Tyler stared in open disbelief. "No," he whispered.

He moved forward quickly now, scanning the ground for any sign of the massive structure that had dominated the summit only hours earlier. There should've been debris everywhere. Charred beams. Twisted iron. Burned stone foundations.

Instead he found nothing. No driveway. No broken glass. No crater. Not even blackened earth where the explosion occurred. The entire mountaintop looked untouched.

He walked faster, heart hammering harder with every step. He crossed the area where the grand entrance should've stood. Nothing. He paced the full width of the hill searching desperately for some evidence he hadn't lost his mind.

Then he spotted something near the tree line. A small, weathered post protruded from the grass. Mounted to it sat a tarnished bronze plaque stained green around the edges from decades of rain and exposure. He approached slowly. The inscription read:

WALNUT LODGE

DEDICATED TO THOSE WHO PERISHED ON THE NIGHT OF JUNE 11, 1930.

WALNUT LODGE WAS A LUXURIOUS RETREAT FREQUENTED BY NOTABLE FIGURES INCLUDING RUDOLPH VALENTINO AND THEDA BARA. POLITICIANS, INDUSTRIALISTS, AND WEALTHY FAMILIES ONCE GATHERED WITHIN THE STATELY MANOR ATOP WALNUT HILL.

OWNER AND RAILROAD MAGNATE CHARLES WORTHINGTON III PERISHED ALONGSIDE NUMEROUS GUESTS DURING A TRAGIC FIRE. FAULTY WIRING AND STRUCTURAL DEFECTS WERE BLAMED.

AN OVERLOADED ELEVATOR COLLAPSED INTO THE BASEMENT BOILER SYSTEM, IGNITING A CATASTROPHIC GAS EXPLOSION WHICH DESTROYED THE ESTATE. VISITORS MAY STILL FIND FRAGMENTS OF THE ORIGINAL STRUCTURE SCATTERED THROUGHOUT THE SURROUNDING AREA. FEEL FREE TO TAKE HOME A PIECE OF HISTORY AND HELP KEEP OUR BEAUTIFUL PARK CLEAN.

He stared at the plaque without moving. *June 11, 1930.* The elevator. The boiler. Charles Worthington III. The fire. Every detail matched. His pulse began hammering painfully in his throat. All of it had already happened. Nearly a century ago.

He slowly backed away from the plaque, mind struggling desperately to force logic into place. Head trauma maybe. Hallucinations after the fall. Some kind of psychological break triggered by stress and exhaustion. Then his boot struck something hidden in the grass. He looked down.

A crude wooden cross stood beside the memorial post, made from two rough boards nailed together. A faded scrap of cardboard hung near the top beneath water-stained tape.

Tyler crouched carefully beside it. The handwriting had nearly washed away completely. But he could still read it.

MICHAEL MCKINNEY
B. 1970 — D.?
DISAPPEARED WHILE HIKING IN 2008.
LAST SEEN HIKING HERE.

He felt the blood drain from his face. The plaque offered explanation. The cross destroyed it.

Michael had been real. Not imagined. Not dreamed. He stood abruptly and staggered downhill toward the lake below the ridge. His thoughts spiraled uselessly now while sunlight flashed through the trees around him. The water appeared moments later through breaks in the forest, calm and silver beneath the morning sky.

He reached the shoreline breathing hard. The lake looked perfectly ordinary too. Still. Beautiful. Unmoved by memory. He almost laughed then. A tired, broken sound caught somewhere between panic and disbelief.

Maybe the mountain had finally scrambled his brain after all. Maybe he lay unconscious somewhere at the bottom of Samson's Cliff right now imagining the entire thing while dying slowly in the woods.

Then something pressed heavily against his thigh. He froze. Slowly, he reached into his pocket. His fingers closed around cold metal. He pulled out a brass room key. The diamond-shaped tortoiseshell tag swung gently beneath the sunlight while black engraved lettering gleamed across its surface.

Room 103 — Walnut Lodge

He numbly stared at it. Dreams didn't leave souvenirs. His breathing grew shallow. Slowly, he looked down toward the water. Then froze completely. The reflection staring back at him wasn't his own. The bellboy gazed upward from the lake surface instead.

Pale face. Perfect hair. That same sharp impossible smile. "There's room for one more," the reflection said softly.

He screamed and kicked violently at the water. The lake exploded into ripples, shattering the image instantly. He stumbled backward across the shoreline, pulse roaring in his ears while water splashed across his boots and jeans. Then he noticed something beneath the surface near the shore. A faint white shape resting in the mud.

Still breathing hard, he crouched carefully and reached into the icy water up to his elbow. His fingers brushed smooth porcelain. He pulled slowly. A white Venetian mask emerged dripping from the lake.

Thea's.

Even half-coated in mud and algae, he recognized it instantly. The tattered black ribbons still clung to the edges while tiny silver cracks spiderwebbed across the pale surface.

He stared at it silently. Then whispered a quiet prayer beneath his breath. For Thea. For Michael. For all of them trapped inside whatever the Walnut Lodge truly was. He rose slowly from the shoreline, water dripping from the ruined mask in his hand.

That was when he noticed something farther up the hill. A backpack. Brown canvas stained with mud. His backpack.

He approached it cautiously as though afraid it might disappear before he reached it. He'd left it inside Room 103 beside the dresser before the explosion. Yet here it sat untouched in the grass beneath the morning sun.

Waiting for him. He knelt beside it carefully and opened the zipper. Everything remained inside. His flashlight. Water bottle. Guidebook. First-aid kit. Even the granola bars he'd packed before the hike. He closed the bag slowly.

Michael McKinney never left that lodge. Neither had Thea. And for one terrible flickering moment, he found himself wondering what might've happened if he'd stayed inside the elevator with them. Would he have died? Or would he simply have become part of the cycle too?

The thought followed him as he slung the backpack over one shoulder and turned away from the lake. Morning sunlight filtered warmly through the forest while birds continued singing overhead, utterly indifferent to the horrors buried beneath the mountain.

The Walnut Lodge was gone. As though it had never existed at all. Yet the brass key still gleamed in Tyler's hand as he started back down the trail. And somewhere deep inside him, beneath the fear and confusion and exhaustion, a quiet voice whispered softly:

It isn't over yet.

Chapter 10

He reached home shortly after noon the next day. The drive back from Roan Mountain passed in a blur of exhaustion and caffeine. He barely remembered half of it. The roads unwound beneath his tires while Appalachian ridges rolled past beneath low gray clouds, and several times he caught himself gripping the steering wheel too tightly without realizing it.

His body still hurt from the fall. Every bruise had stiffened overnight. Worse than the pain, though, was the strange disconnected feeling that clung to him since leaving the mountain, like part of his mind still wandered those upper halls beneath the Walnut Lodge.

By the time he pulled into the gravel driveway outside his house in Johnson City, he felt hollowed out. Home looked painfully ordinary. A half-dead fern drooped beside the porch steps. Someone nearby mowed their lawn while country music drifted faintly across the neighborhood. A pair of kids rode bicycles near the corner mailbox without a care in the world. After everything he'd seen on the mountain, normal life felt surreal in its own way.

He shut off the engine and sat there for a long moment. Then he looked at the brass key resting in the passenger seat. *Room 103.* The Walnut Lodge.

Even now, sunlight gleamed across the tarnished metal exactly the same way it had beside the lake. Tyler picked it up carefully, turning it between his fingers before finally shoving it into his jacket pocket. He didn't know why he kept carrying it. Maybe because throwing it away felt dangerous.

Inside, the house smelled faintly stale from being empty for several days. He dropped his backpack beside the couch and stood quietly in the living room listening to the silence around him. The television remote still sat exactly where he'd left it. Dirty dishes waited in the sink. Leigh's coffee mug remained beside the Keurig with a fading lipstick mark still clinging to the rim.

The sight of it exhausted him instantly. The mountain had stripped something loose inside him. Before the trip, he might've avoided the confrontation another few weeks. Maybe another month. Pretended not to notice the lies. Pretended not to care where Leigh disappeared every weekend.

Now the thought of continuing the relationship felt unbearable. Too much falseness already haunted his life. He pulled out his phone and stared at her contact information for nearly a minute before finally pressing call.

The line rang twice.

"Hey, stranger," Leigh answered brightly. "You survive the wilderness?"

Tyler closed his eyes briefly. The casual warmth in her voice irritated him more than anger would have. "Yeah," he said quietly. "I made it back."

"You sound tired."

"I am."

A pause settled briefly between them.

"You okay?" she asked.

The concern sounded practiced now. Rehearsed. Tyler walked slowly toward the kitchen window while gathering his thoughts. Outside, wind stirred softly through the trees lining the backyard. "No," he admitted finally. "I don't think I am."

Another silence followed. "What happened?"

How could he even begin answering that question? *I got trapped in a haunted hotel from 1930 filled with dead people reenacting their own deaths every night.* Instead he said, "I've had a lot of time to think."

She didn't respond immediately. That alone told him she already knew where the conversation was heading.

"I called Stacy," he said. The silence afterward stretched longer this time. Finally she sighed softly into the phone.

"Tyler…"

"She's not sick."

"I can explain."

"You've had months to explain." His voice remained calmer than he expected. Not cold exactly. Just tired. Completely tired.

She tried anyway. Half-finished excuses spilled through the phone. Stress. Confusion. Feeling trapped. Not knowing how to tell him things had changed. Tyler barely listened. The words washed over him meaninglessly while his eyes drifted toward the dark reflection hanging in the kitchen window glass.

For one brief second, he thought someone stood behind him. A pale figure. Perfectly still. He turned immediately. The kitchen stood empty. His pulse jumped hard anyway.

"You still there?" Leigh asked.

"Yeah."

"You're scaring me."

The irony almost made him laugh. He rubbed one hand across his eyes. "I'm done, Leigh."

The words settled heavily between them. No yelling followed. No dramatic explosion. Just quiet. And somehow that hurt more.

"You don't mean that," she whispered finally.

"I do." Another long pause.

Then her voice softened into something fragile and unfamiliar. "Did somebody else happen?"

Tyler thought immediately of Thea. The white mask. The dancing. Her hand gripping his inside the ballroom while the orchestra thundered endlessly around them.

"No," he answered truthfully. "Something happened. But not that."

Leigh sounded close to tears now. "Can we at least talk in person?"

"Maybe later," Tyler said. "I just need… space right now." He ended the call before she could answer. The silence afterward felt enormous. He lowered the phone slowly and leaned against the kitchen counter while exhaustion settled over him all over again. Part of him expected relief after finally ending things with her. Instead he mostly felt numb.

His gaze drifted unconsciously toward the hallway leading deeper into the house. Something moved. Fast. Like a figure disappearing around the corner. He straightened immediately. "Hello?"

Nothing answered. He stepped carefully into the hallway, pulse quickening despite himself. Sunlight spilled dimly through the blinds across the bedroom door and bathroom entrance. Everything looked normal. Empty. Still.

"You're losing it," he muttered under his breath. Stress. That's all this was. Stress, exhaustion, trauma, dehydration, maybe even a mild concussion from the mountain. People hallucinated after things like that. His brain simply hadn't caught up with reality yet.

Tyler returned slowly to the kitchen. The brass key still rested in his jacket pocket. Heavy. Cold. He pulled it out again and laid it carefully on the counter beside the sink. The metal clink echoed strangely loud through the quiet house.

For a moment, he simply stared at it. Then the lights flickered. Once. Twice. The kitchen dimmed briefly before returning to normal. He frowned upward toward the ceiling fixture.

"Great." Probably the storm system moving through the mountains. The power grid around here flickered every time somebody sneezed too hard near a transformer.

Still… A faint smell lingered suddenly in the kitchen air. Not electrical smoke. Something else. Gasoline maybe. No. Gas. Tyler's stomach tightened immediately. The boiler room. The elevator shaft.

He looked around quickly and moved toward the stove, checking the burners one by one. Everything sat firmly off. No hiss escaped the lines. The smell faded almost as quickly as it appeared.

His nerves were catching up with him. He opened the refrigerator and grabbed a bottle of water with shaking hands. The cold helped steady him a little. He took several long drinks before forcing himself to breathe normally again.

"You survived a fall," he muttered. "A breakup. Probably a concussion. That's all this is." But even as he said it, his eyes drifted back toward the brass key. The overhead light flickered again. And somewhere deep inside the house, very faintly, he thought he heard distant music. Trumpets. Laughter.

Then silence once more.

Chapter 11

Leigh chose the restaurant. Of course she did. Tyler sat alone in a booth near the back wall of a softly lit Italian place downtown, listening to muted jazz drift through hidden speakers while rain crawled slowly down the front windows outside. The entire place smelled like garlic, wine, and baked bread. Couples filled most of the booths around him, leaning close across candlelight and half-finished meals while waiters drifted between tables carrying steaming plates.

The normalcy of it all felt distant now. Like watching someone else's life through thick glass. He checked his phone again, 7:32. Leigh was late.

Not dramatically late. Just enough to remind him of every other night spent waiting on vague excuses and apologetic texts. He leaned back in the booth and rubbed at the bruise still lingering beneath his ribs. The ache had settled deep into his body now, constant and dull. Sometimes it almost felt like the mountain itself remained lodged inside him somewhere.

Then the restaurant door opened. She stepped inside shaking rainwater from her coat. For a brief moment, seeing her still hit him the old way. Familiarity. Attraction. History. She wore the same dark green sweater he always liked on her, her auburn hair falling loose around her shoulders while silver earrings caught the warm restaurant light. Anybody looking at them from across the room would've assumed they were an ordinary couple meeting for dinner after work.

He knew better now. She spotted him and approached carefully.

"You look awful," she said softly as she slid into the booth opposite him.

"Good to see you too."

"I mean it." Concern flickered across her face. "You look exhausted."

Tyler almost laughed. Exhausted didn't begin covering it. The waitress arrived before either could continue, awkwardly cheerful while asking about drinks. Tyler ordered coffee. Leigh requested wine. Once the waitress disappeared again, silence settled heavily between them.

Leigh folded her hands together atop the table. "So," she said carefully. "Are you going to tell me what actually happened up there?"

Tyler stared at her for several seconds before answering. "No."

Her expression tightened slightly. "Tyler—"

"You lied to me for months." The words landed flat and cold between them.

She looked away first. People always did when the truth finally arrived. "I know," she admitted quietly.

"No, I don't think you do." The jazz music drifting through the restaurant suddenly reminded him faintly of the ballroom orchestra at Walnut Lodge. The realization made his stomach tighten instantly. She glanced toward the speakers overhead until the feeling passed.

Leigh leaned forward slightly. "I never meant for things to get this far."

"That's what everybody says after they get caught."

"It wasn't like that."

Tyler shook his head slowly. "You know what the worst part is?"

She didn't answer.

"I spent months convincing myself I was paranoid." He looked down briefly at his coffee cup after the waitress set it in front of him. Steam curled upward between them. "Every time something felt wrong, I explained it away. I defended you to myself."

Her eyes glistened slightly now. "I didn't want to hurt you."

"That stopped being true a long time ago." The words hurt him too. More than he expected.

She sat quietly for a moment, staring down at the tablecloth while rain tapped softly against the windows outside. When she finally spoke again, her voice sounded smaller somehow.

"There is someone else."

Tyler nodded once. "I figured."

"It wasn't supposed to happen."

"That's usually how affairs work." She flinched visibly at the word.

Good. Part of him wanted her uncomfortable. Not devastated exactly. Just forced to sit honestly inside the damage for once instead of floating around it through excuses and soft language.

"How long?" he asked.

"A few months." Longer than she admitted, probably. He sipped the coffee carefully, though it tasted bitter and burnt. Across the restaurant, somebody laughed loudly near the bar. Glasses clinked together. Normal life carried on around them while his own quietly collapsed.

Oddly enough, he didn't feel angry anymore. The Walnut Lodge had burned something out of him.

"You should've just left," he said quietly.

She wiped at one eye. "I was trying to figure things out."

"No. You were trying to keep both lives at once."

Silence again. This time she didn't argue. Tyler leaned back slowly against the booth. "I'm not doing this anymore, Leigh."

Her eyes lifted toward him. "So that's it?"

"Yes."

"You really mean it?"

He nodded.

For a second, genuine grief crossed her face. Not manipulative. Not theatrical. Real sadness finally breaking through after the lies lost their usefulness. And somehow that made everything worse.

"I did love you," she whispered.

He thought about Thea's hand in his. The ballroom. The elevator. The screams. Then he thought about the bellboy smiling through the fire while the lodge exploded behind him.

"There are worse things than losing somebody," he said quietly.

She frowned faintly. "What does that mean?"

He stared past her toward the rain-dark windows. "I'm not really sure anymore."

They finished the conversation quietly after that. Logistics mostly. Picking up belongings. Untangling routines. Practical things people discussed while pretending heartbreak could be organized neatly into boxes and schedules.

When they finally stood outside beneath the restaurant awning, rain still fell steadily across downtown. She looked at him one last time. "You really aren't coming back from whatever happened on that mountain, are you?"

The question unsettled him because it sounded less emotional than observant. He forced a tired smile. "Probably not."

Then she kissed his cheek softly and walked away into the rain. He watched her disappear down the sidewalk without following. And realized he felt more haunted than heartbroken.

By the time he returned home, the rain had deepened into a steady storm rattling softly against the house windows. He tossed his keys onto the kitchen counter and stood quietly in the dark listening to the house settle around him.

Empty now. Her absence already felt physical somehow. The silence reminded him too much of the lodge.

He immediately turned on the television just for noise. Some late-night sitcom filled the living room with canned laughter while he showered and changed clothes, but even from the bathroom he kept hearing other sounds beneath it.

Faint music. Footsteps upstairs. The distant metallic groan of elevator cables. Every time he checked, the house sat empty. Eventually exhaustion dragged him into bed sometime after midnight.

Sleep came hard and fast. And the dreams returned immediately. He stood once more inside the Walnut Lodge ballroom beneath blazing chandeliers and endless music. Dancers spun around him in slow elegant circles while champagne glasses flashed beneath golden light. The orchestra played something distant and warped now, notes dragging strangely like an old phonograph turning too slowly.

The ballroom looked damaged. Burn marks crawled across the ceiling frescoes overhead. Smoke stains blackened the marble columns. Several guests drifted through the crowd with dark scorch marks climbing their clothing and necks.

Yet nobody acknowledged it. They kept dancing. Kept smiling. Kept drinking. Then he saw Thea. She stood alone near the far end of the ballroom wearing the same black dress and white Venetian mask. But now soot streaked one side of her face beneath the mask, and part of her hair looked burned away entirely.

"Thea!" She looked toward him instantly. Relief flooded her eyes. He pushed through the dancers trying to reach her, but the crowd moved strangely around him, bodies sliding endlessly between them no matter how fast he walked. The orchestra grew louder. Guests laughed too hard. Somewhere nearby, somebody screamed inside the music. Ash rained down on dancers and musicians alike.

"Thea!" She opened her mouth. At first he couldn't understand the words. The sound arrived muffled, distant beneath the orchestra and roaring fire. Then one word broke through clearly.

"Return."

Tyler stopped. "What?"

Thea reached toward him desperately now. "Return!"

The ballroom lights flickered violently. Suddenly the music warped into screams. Fire burst through the walls. Guests continued dancing while flames consumed them.

He woke violently in bed gasping for breath. The bedroom stood dark except for pale moonlight leaking through the blinds. Rain hammered the windows outside. His heart pounded painfully against his ribs while the word still echoed through his mind.

Return. He sat upright breathing hard and rubbed both hands over his face. "She wants me to go back," he whispered.

The idea sounded insane. But what else could it mean? Thea was trapped there somehow. Michael too. Maybe all of them were. The lodge still existed in some impossible way beyond the mountain and time and fire, repeating itself endlessly every night. And now it wanted him back.

He swung his legs over the side of the bed and stood shakily. That's all this is, he told himself. Trauma dreams. Survivor's guilt. Stress. Except the bedroom smelled faintly of smoke. He froze. Not cigarette smoke. Burning wood. Burning fabric. The exact smell from the exploding ballroom.

Slowly, he turned toward the bedroom doorway. A wet set of footprints crossed the hallway carpet outside. He stared in horror. Water rippled softly in each print. One after another. Leading toward the living room.

He grabbed the baseball bat leaning beside the dresser and stepped cautiously into the hall. The footprints continued through the dark house, glistening faintly beneath flashes of stormlight from the windows.

Toward the kitchen. Toward the back door. He rounded the corner gripping the bat tightly. Nobody stood there. The kitchen sat empty. But water pooled quietly across the tile floor near the sink.

And resting beside the puddle… was the white Venetian mask.

Chapter 12

Rain hung low over Johnson City the next morning. It turned the streets silver beneath a blanket of cold Appalachian fog. He drove across town in silence with Leigh's belongings stacked in cardboard boxes across the back seat of his truck. Every bump in the road shifted something behind him, hangers clacking softly against one another while framed photographs slid inside loose newspaper wrapping.

The domestic normalcy of it all felt surreal. A week ago, he would've imagined this moment differently. Angrier maybe. Dramatic. He'd pictured shouting matches, slammed doors, accusations hurled across parking lots like broken glass. Instead he mostly felt numb, moving through the breakup with the detached exhaustion of someone handling funeral arrangements.

Leigh's mother lived in a quiet brick ranch house near Elizabethton surrounded by old maple trees already beginning to yellow at the edges despite the lingering summer heat. He parked beside the curb and sat staring through the rain-speckled windshield for a long moment before finally climbing out.

The brass room key rested in his pocket. He carried it everywhere now. Without understanding why. Leigh opened the front door before he even reached the porch. Her eyes looked swollen and tired, dark circles lingering beneath them like bruises.

She wore leggings and an oversized sweatshirt with damp hair pulled hastily into a knot, looking less like the polished version of herself he'd grown used to and more like somebody stripped raw by several sleepless nights. Neither of them spoke immediately.

"I brought your stuff," Tyler said finally.

Leigh nodded quietly. "Thanks."

Together they carried the boxes inside while rain tapped steadily against the porch roof overhead. Her mother remained somewhere deeper in the house pretending politely not to intrude, though he occasionally caught movement beyond the hallway as she peeked toward the living room.

Leigh set the last box beside the couch and folded her arms tightly across herself. "I found an apartment," she said after a while.

Tyler looked up. "Already?"

"It's temporary." She shrugged weakly. "Small place near Bristol. Month-to-month lease."

He nodded once. "Okay."

Silence settled between them again. It no longer felt hostile. Just finished.

Leigh glanced toward him carefully. "You still look awful."

"Getting that a lot lately."

"I'm serious." She stepped closer, concern creeping visibly across her face again. "You've lost weight in like three days. And your eyes...."

He instinctively looked away. Sleep hadn't really existed since the mountain. Only brief stretches of unconsciousness broken by fire, music, and Thea's voice echoing endlessly through his dreams. Return. Always the same word. Always spoken with growing urgency.

"I'm fine," he lied.

She studied him for several seconds. "You keep doing that thing."

"What thing?"

"Looking over your shoulder."

The observation unsettled him because he hadn't realized he was doing it. He rubbed one hand across the back of his neck. "Just tired."

She hesitated. Then quietly asked, "Did somebody die up there?"

The question hit harder than expected. His mind flashed instantly to the elevator shaft. Burning guests trapped beneath twisted iron while the boiler roared underneath them. Thea reaching toward him through smoke and fire.

He swallowed hard. "I don't know," he answered honestly.

Leigh frowned slightly. "What does that mean?"

"It means I honestly don't know anymore. I just had a bad fall, alone. Really puts your priorities in perspective."

Rain intensified briefly outside, drumming against the windows while somewhere deeper in the house an old clock chimed softly. He suddenly became aware of faint music drifting through the room. Big band music. Trumpets. Piano. His pulse jumped violently. He turned quickly toward the hallway. Nothing. Only silence.

"You okay?" Leigh asked quietly.

Tyler forced himself to breathe normally again. "Yeah." But he wasn't. Because for half a second, he could've sworn he saw Thea standing at the far end of the hallway behind Leigh's shoulder. White mask. Black dress. One pale hand reaching toward him. *Return.*

The word brushed softly through his mind. Then she vanished. He stepped backward immediately. "I should go."

Leigh looked startled. "Tyler—"

"I mean it. I just… I need to go." He barely waited for a response before heading toward the front door. She followed him onto the porch while rain drifted cold through the gray morning air.

"Whatever happened up there," she said softly, "you should talk to somebody."

Tyler almost laughed. Who exactly? A therapist? Hi, yes, I visited a ghost hotel from 1930, and now dead people keep following me home. Instead he simply nodded and climbed back into the truck. As he pulled away from the curb, he glanced once in the rearview mirror.

She still stood on the porch watching him leave. And beside her, for one impossible instant, stood the bellboy. Perfectly still beneath the rain. Smiling.

He slammed on the brakes hard enough the truck fishtailed slightly across the wet road. The porch stood empty except for Leigh. The bellboy was gone. He drove to work shaking.

The publishing warehouse smelled like cardboard, printer ink, and overheated machinery. Normally the familiarity grounded him. Rows of stacked shipments, buzzing fluorescent lights, coworkers complaining about deadlines and damaged orders. Simple ordinary life.

Today it all felt distant. Muted. Tyler sat through half the morning staring blankly at his computer screen while emails piled up unanswered. His boss stopped twice to ask if he needed to go home sick. Tyler insisted he was fine both times.

He wasn't fooling anybody. By lunch, the headaches started again. A dull pressure built behind his eyes while strange sounds drifted in and out beneath the normal office noise. Sometimes he heard elevator cables creaking somewhere overhead. Other times faint jazz music threaded itself through the hum of fluorescent lights and air conditioning vents.

Once he distinctly heard laughter echo from the copy room, low and muffled like guests talking behind closed doors, only to find the room completely empty when he checked. The first phone call came shortly after two. He frowned at the display on his desk phone.

No number. No caller ID. Just blank static where information should've been. Probably spam. Still, unease tightened low in his stomach as he picked up the receiver.

"Hello?"

At first he heard nothing except faint static crackling softly through the line. Then came music. Old music.

Distant brass instruments drifting somewhere far away beneath layers of interference. The sound resembled an ancient radio station bleeding weakly through a storm. He sat upright slowly.

"Hello?" More sounds emerged beneath the static.

Glasses clinking. Soft laughter. The muffled swell of an orchestra somewhere enormous and crowded. Then a woman's voice whispered faintly through the noise.

"Tyler..."

His blood ran cold. "Thea?"

The line crackled violently for a second before her voice returned again, weak and broken by static. "...return..." Then silence. The connection died completely.

He stared at the phone in his hand while cold prickled slowly across his arms. Across the cubicles, Amanda looked up from her computer with concern written across her face.

"You okay?"

He swallowed hard. "Did you hear that?"

"Hear what?"

"Music."

Amanda frowned. "I didn't hear anything."

He looked slowly back toward the receiver. The caller ID screen remained completely blank. No incoming number. No missed call record. Nothing. As though the phone had never rung at all.

The second call arrived less than an hour later. This time he answered immediately. "What do you want?"

Static hissed softly through the line. Then the orchestra returned, louder now. Not muffled and distant anymore. Closer. Clear enough that he could distinguish trumpets beneath the piano and upright bass. Somewhere inside the noise, guests laughed. Then came another sound.

The elevator. He recognized it instantly. The groaning cables. The grinding gears. Metal straining under impossible weight.

Panic fluttered sharply through his chest while voices drifted beneath the machinery, half drowned by static and music.

"We're trapped!"

"The door won't open!"

Then Thea again. Closer this time. Desperate. "Return…"

The word stretched strangely through the receiver, warping beneath static until it almost sounded like multiple voices speaking together. "Return…"

He gripped the edge of the desk hard enough his knuckles whitened.

"What do you want from me?" he whispered. The orchestra swelled louder. Somewhere beyond it, he thought he heard the bellboy laughing softly.

Then the line went dead again. He remained frozen at his desk long after the silence returned. Fluorescent lights buzzed overhead while coworkers moved through the office carrying coffee cups and paperwork, completely unaware that something impossible had just reached through the phone line searching for him. Because now he understood something truly horrifying.

The Walnut Lodge wasn't staying on the mountain. Little by little, piece by piece, it was beginning to follow him home.

Chapter 13

He stopped using elevators two days later. At first he told himself it was practical. After watching a packed elevator car plunge through the center of the Walnut Lodge and explode into fire beneath the mountain, avoiding them seemed like a perfectly reasonable trauma response.

Nobody would blame him for taking the stairs at work or choosing escalators at stores. But deep down, he knew it was more than that. Elevators felt wrong now. Alive somehow.

Every metallic groan of cables overhead tightened something instinctive inside his chest. Every closing set of doors looked less like machinery and more like a mouth preparing to swallow him whole. By Thursday morning, he had begun studying elevator operators in old photographs online.

Not intentionally. It simply happened. He sat at his desk pretending to answer emails while another browser window remained open beside his work software, filled with grainy black-and-white images from the early twentieth century. Bellboys. Hotel attendants. Elevator operators standing stiffly beside brass gates with gloved hands folded neatly behind their backs.

Every single photograph unsettled him. Not because any matched exactly. Because all of them almost did. The same posture. The same fixed politeness. The same strange artificial warmth. Tyler closed the browser hard enough to make Amanda glance over from the neighboring cubicle.

"You sure you're okay?"

"Fine."

"You've said 'fine' like six times today."

He rubbed both hands over his face. Sleep had abandoned him almost completely now. The nightmares grew worse every night, and exhaustion hollowed him out more with every passing hour. Dark circles hung beneath his eyes. His nerves felt stretched painfully tight.

Worst of all, Thea's voice had changed. At first the dreams frightened him because they felt mournful. Now they felt urgent.

The Lodge no longer appeared merely haunted in his sleep. It looked unstable. Sick. Corridors warped and stretched impossibly into darkness. Ballroom walls blackened with spreading burn marks. Music slowed and distorted like dying phonograph records while guests continued dancing through smoke and falling ash.

And always, somewhere in the middle of it all, Thea searched for him. *Return.* The word followed him constantly. Sometimes whispered softly inside dreams. Sometimes echoing through static-filled phone calls.

Once, horrifyingly, he'd heard it whispered directly beside his ear while standing alone in his kitchen. He grabbed his coffee and forced himself back toward work. Numbers blurred meaninglessly across spreadsheets while the office hummed around him beneath buzzing fluorescent lights. Around noon, he volunteered to carry inventory forms downstairs just for an excuse to move.

The stairwell felt safer than the elevator. At least until he reached the third-floor landing. He stopped abruptly. The wallpaper had changed. His pulse stumbled hard. Only for a second. Only along one section of the hallway visible through the stairwell door window. But it had definitely changed. Gone was the ordinary beige office wallpaper. In its place stretched dark burgundy fabric patterned with twisting gold vines.

Walnut Lodge wallpaper.

He stared in disbelief. The hallway beyond even looked dimmer somehow, lit with softer amber light instead of harsh office fluorescents. Then somebody laughed nearby.

The sound snapped reality back into place instantly. Normal office walls returned. Cheap beige paint now. Industrial lighting. Nothing else.

He backed slowly down the stairwell gripping the railing tightly. "No," he whispered. "No, no…" People didn't hallucinate entire architectural changes. Did they? Or maybe they did.

By late afternoon, he finally left work early pretending migraine symptoms. Nobody argued. His boss looked relieved more than concerned. He had spent most of the day distracted and pale, repeatedly staring into corners like somebody expecting movement.

The drive home unsettled him even worse. At a stoplight near downtown, he glanced absently toward the hotel across the street. And saw the Bellboy standing beneath the awning.

Rain drifted softly through gray afternoon fog while traffic hissed along wet pavement between them. The Bellboy stood perfectly still near the revolving doors, dressed in the same immaculate uniform from Walnut Lodge. Pale gloves. Brass buttons. That same impossible smile.

Watching him. His hands locked around the steering wheel. Cars honked behind him as the light turned green. The Bellboy tipped his head politely. Then vanished behind passing traffic.

He nearly ran the next red light. By the time he reached home, rain had intensified into a cold steady drizzle that soaked the sidewalks and windows alike. He hurried inside, locked the door behind him, and immediately froze.

Music drifted softly through the house. Big band music. Clear this time. Not faint. Not imagined. Tyler moved cautiously toward the living room. The television sat off. The kitchen remained empty. But somewhere deeper in the house, muted trumpets and piano played softly beneath the rainstorm outside.

His eyes drifted toward the hallway. Light spilled beneath the bedroom door. Warm golden light. Not the bluish lamp he normally used. Ballroom light.

His pulse hammered violently now. Slowly, he approached the bedroom. The music grew louder with every step. Laughter followed it. Crystal glasses clinking together. The low murmur of dozens of distant voices.

His hand shook as he reached for the doorknob. Then the phone rang. The sound exploded through the house hard enough to make him jump. He spun toward the kitchen counter where his cell phone vibrated loudly against the surface.

Unknown Caller. No number attached. Just blankness. The music from the bedroom stopped instantly. Silence crashed over the house. He stared at the phone for several long seconds before finally answering. "Hello…?"

Static crackled softly through the line. Then came the Bellboy's voice. "Good evening, Mr. Mercer." His blood froze. The voice sounded perfectly calm. Perfectly polite. As though calling to confirm a dinner reservation.

Tyler swallowed hard. "Who are you?"

A soft chuckle drifted through the receiver. "You've checked in, sir."

The smell of smoke crept suddenly through the house. Tyler looked slowly toward the hallway. The bedroom light glowed faint amber beneath the door again.

"What do you want from me?" Tyler whispered.

"We simply wish to accommodate our guests." Something moved beneath the bedroom door. A shadow. Two feet crossing slowly through the warm light.

He backed away. "You're not real."

The Bellboy laughed softly again. "Oh, but we are very real, sir." His voice lowered slightly. "More and more every evening."

His stomach dropped. The hallway walls creaked softly. Then came another sound. The distant metallic groan of elevator cables somewhere inside the house walls. Slowly. Patiently. Drawing closer.

"You've taken something belonging to the Lodge," the Bellboy continued pleasantly. "And the Lodge would very much like it returned."

The brass key suddenly felt ice cold inside Tyler's pocket. Before he could answer, the line filled abruptly with orchestra music so loud it distorted the speaker. Guests laughed wildly somewhere beyond it while elevator machinery screamed beneath the noise.

Then came Thea's voice. Closer than ever before. Terrified. "Tyler, return the key!"

The line went dead. At that exact moment, the bedroom door slowly creaked open by itself.

Chapter 14

He barely slept after the bedroom door opened. He never actually saw anyone standing there. That somehow made it worse. The hallway beyond remained empty except for darkness and the faint yellow glow leaking from the kitchen. Yet the bedroom door had opened slowly, deliberately, as though somebody unseen had turned the knob from the other side.

He spent the rest of the night sitting on the couch with every light in the house turned on and a baseball bat resting across his knees. Around three in the morning, exhaustion finally dragged him into a shallow half-sleep filled with broken dreams and drifting music.

Thea appeared again. This time she stood beside the lake beneath the mountain instead of inside the ballroom. Fog rolled heavily across the shoreline while moonlight shimmered silver across perfectly still water. The white Venetian mask hung loose in one hand now, exposing the soot-blackened burns climbing the left side of her face and neck.

She looked frightened. Not ghostly. Not monstrous. Just frightened. He moved toward her through the fog while distant orchestra music drifted faintly through the trees somewhere behind them. "Thea."

Her eyes fixed desperately on him. She tried speaking. He saw the words forming clearly on her lips now. Fast. Urgent. Pleading. But once again, only one word reached him. "Return."

Tyler stopped in frustration. "No," he snapped. "I don't understand what you mean."

She stepped closer. Behind her, movement stirred faintly in the fog surrounding the lake. Figures drifted there beneath the trees. Guests from the Lodge standing motionless in evening clothes while smoke curled faintly around them.

Then the Bellboy appeared among them. Perfectly still. Watching. Thea turned immediately toward him in terror. "Return!" she cried again. This time her voice cracked with panic. The Bellboy smiled. Then he woke gasping on the couch beneath the harsh glow of the living room lamp.

Morning sunlight spilled weakly through the blinds. The television played infomercials softly to itself. His neck and back screamed from sleeping upright. And resting on the coffee table directly in front of him sat the brass room key.

He stared at it numbly. He knew for a fact he'd left it in the kitchen. Slowly, he picked it up. The metal felt colder than ever. By noon, the idea of returning to Roan Mountain had rooted itself firmly enough in his mind that he couldn't ignore it anymore. He paced the house restlessly while rain clouds drifted low across the hills outside, replaying Thea's voice over and over again in his head.

Return. Maybe she wanted help. Maybe something inside the Lodge remained trapped. Or maybe the Bellboy simply wanted him back there permanently.

That possibility kept stopping him cold every time he considered grabbing his keys and driving toward the mountain. Because the Bellboy no longer felt like a ghost. He felt intentional. Aware.

He stood in the kitchen staring absently out the window when movement across the street caught his eye. The Bellboy stood at the bus stop. Rain mist drifted softly around him while passing cars hissed through wet pavement nearby. He wore the same immaculate uniform from the Lodge. Pale gloves folded neatly behind his back while he watched the house from beneath the shelter awning.

Nobody around him seemed to notice anything strange. A teenager sat nearby scrolling through her phone. An older couple waited beneath umbrellas. The Bellboy stood among them smiling faintly like he belonged there.

He stumbled backward from the window. When he looked again seconds later, the bus stop stood empty. His pulse hammered painfully.

"This is stress," he muttered aloud. "Trauma. Sleep deprivation." The words sounded weak now. He no longer fully believed them himself.

By afternoon, he finally decided he needed answers more than reassurance. If the Walnut Lodge truly existed, there had to be records somewhere beyond that tiny plaque on the mountain. Old newspapers. Photographs. Death certificates. Something.

He opened his laptop and began searching. At first, results appeared sparse and oddly inconsistent. Most searches only produced brief references to a 1930 fire near Roan Mountain. Some articles referred to Walnut Lodge as a hotel. Others called it a private estate or retreat. Several records contradicted one another outright.

One article claimed 23 guests died. Another listed 81. One insisted the building collapsed entirely during the fire. Another stated much of the structure remained standing for years afterward. He frowned harder as he dug deeper. Nothing aligned cleanly. Even stranger, many search results disappeared after he clicked them. Entire archived pages failed to load. Photographs corrupted halfway through opening.

One historical society website simply redirected him repeatedly to unrelated railroad articles no matter how many times he searched Walnut Lodge directly.

It felt less like missing history and more like history actively resisting him. Eventually he found an old black-and-white photograph buried inside a forgotten university archive.

The image showed Walnut Lodge sometime during the late 1920s. He stared at it breathlessly. The building looked exactly as he remembered. Towering columns. Massive ballroom windows. Wide stone terraces overlooking the mountains.

Guests gathered outside in evening attire beneath strings of glowing lanterns while luxury automobiles lined the curved driveway. And standing near the front entrance… the Bellboy.

Tyler leaned closer toward the screen. The photograph quality remained grainy, but there was no mistaking him. Same uniform. Same posture. Same faint smile. Exactly the same. No aging. No difference whatsoever. A cold sensation crawled slowly up Tyler's spine.

He checked the photograph date again. Impossible. Then the image flickered. For one split second, the Bellboy's face changed. Not dramatically. Just enough. The smile widened slightly. His eyes shifted upward. Looking through the screen, directly at Tyler. The laptop snapped shut instantly. He stumbled backward from the table breathing hard.

"Nope." Silence filled the house again. Then somewhere upstairs, despite living in a single-story house, Tyler heard footsteps crossing slowly overhead.

One measured step at a time. Floorboards creaked softly above him. Tyler stared upward in horror. The footsteps continued. Then came another sound. Elevator cables groaned faintly somewhere inside the walls.

The brass key vibrated suddenly in his pocket. Not hard. Just enough to feel. He pulled it out slowly. The engraved numbers looked different now.

Room 103 had become:

GUEST 103

His stomach dropped. A phone rang somewhere nearby. Not his cellphone. Not the television. An old rotary phone.

The sound echoed faintly through the house from somewhere deeper inside the house where no phone should've existed. One ring. Two. Three. He followed the sound slowly down the hallway. The air changed as he walked. Warmer. Thicker. The smell of cigarette smoke and old perfume drifted faintly through the darkness ahead. Another ring echoed softly.

Then another. At the end of the hallway, the bathroom door stood slightly open. Warm golden light spilled through the crack beneath it. Ballroom light. He stopped breathing entirely. Because faintly, somewhere beyond the bathroom door, he heard people laughing.

Chapter 15

His dreams remained strangely quiet that night. No burning ballroom. No screaming elevator cables. No guests dancing through smoke while the orchestra played itself into oblivion. Instead he wandered empty halls.

The Walnut Lodge stretched endlessly around him beneath dim amber lights while distant music drifted somewhere far away behind closed doors. The corridors looked abandoned now, stripped of the manic glamour they once carried. Dust coated the marble floors. Chandeliers hung dark overhead. Torn wallpaper peeled from the walls in long curling strips. Only Thea remained.

He caught glimpses of her throughout the dream, always just ahead of him at the far end of another hallway. She was delicate elegance in corporal form. Sometimes she stood beside windows overlooking black mountains swallowed in fog. Other times she waited beside elevators with one hand pressed anxiously against the brass gates.

Every time he tried reaching her, the Lodge shifted around him. Doors appeared where walls should've been. Hallways bent impossibly. Rooms stretched longer than physics allowed. And always, she kept repeating the same word. "Return."

Not angry. Not commanding. Desperate. The dream finally ended with him standing alone before Room 103. The brass number plaque hung crooked against the door while smoke curled slowly beneath it. Somewhere on the other side, guests laughed softly beneath the sound of distant jazz music.

Then came the Bellboy's voice. Right behind him.

"Some doors should remain closed, sir."

He woke instantly. Gray dawn filtered weakly through the blinds while rain tapped softly against the house windows. For several seconds he simply lay there staring upward at the ceiling, trying to separate dream from reality.

The smell of cigarette smoke lingered faintly in the bedroom. Not strong. But there. He sat up slowly and rubbed sleep from his eyes. Every night the Lodge pushed a little farther into his life. The boundaries separating dreams from waking reality no longer felt reliable. Half the time he genuinely couldn't tell whether something paranormal had happened or whether exhaustion and fear had finally started breaking his mind apart.

He showered quickly and dressed for work while trying hard not to think about the Bellboy standing inside that old photograph from 1928 smiling directly through the computer screen.

By 7:30, he stood in the kitchen pouring stale coffee into a travel mug while local news murmured quietly from the television in the living room. Rain still drifted steadily outside, coating the windows in silver streaks while thunder rolled faintly somewhere deep in the mountains.

The house felt calm for once. Almost normal. That frightened him more than the haunting did. Because Walnut Lodge never stayed quiet long. He screwed the lid onto the travel mug and turned toward the hallway. Then stopped dead.

The Bellboy sat calmly at the kitchen table. His breath caught so hard it hurt. The Bellboy looked perfectly solid in the morning light, dressed in the same immaculate dark uniform with polished brass buttons gleaming softly beneath the overhead fixture.

Pale gloves rested neatly atop the table while one ankle crossed casually over the opposite knee. He might've been mistaken for an ordinary hotel employee waiting politely for instructions if not for the impossible stillness surrounding him.

No movement. No breathing. Just that faint patient smile. He stumbled backward hard enough to slam against the counter. "What the hell—"

"Good morning, Mr. Mercer," the Bellboy said pleasantly. His voice sounded exactly the same as it had over the phone. Smooth. Cultured. Ancient.

His pulse exploded. "You—you're not real."

The Bellboy tilted his head slightly. "An increasingly difficult argument to maintain, sir."

He grabbed the nearest thing within reach, a heavy ceramic mug, and held it like a weapon. The Bellboy didn't react at all. Rain tapped softly against the windows while the kitchen clock ticked behind them. Everything suddenly felt horribly quiet.

"What are you?" Tyler whispered. The Bellboy's smile widened slightly. "A servant."

"Bullshit."

"A host, then, if you prefer."

His hands shook visibly now. "What do you want from me?"

The Bellboy glanced briefly toward Tyler's jacket hanging beside the front door. Toward the brass key inside the pocket. "You have something that belongs to the Lodge."

"Why should I give it to you?"

That actually seemed to amuse him. "Oh no," the Bellboy said softly. "The Lodge does not wish the key returned to me."

He froze. Something cold slid slowly through his stomach.

"Thea," he whispered.

The Bellboy's expression changed almost imperceptibly at the name. Not anger exactly. Irritation. Like a hotel manager forced to acknowledge an unpleasant guest complaint.

"She was always rather difficult," he said lightly.

Tyler gripped the mug harder. "What is she trying to tell me?"

The Bellboy stood slowly from the table. The movement looked wrong somehow, too smooth and deliberate, like something imitating human motion rather than naturally performing it. He adjusted one white glove carefully while studying Tyler with calm pale eyes.

"You've become curious, Mr. Mercer."

"You murdered those people."

The Bellboy laughed softly. "No," he corrected. "They returned. We all return."

The answer chilled Tyler worse than outright violence would've. Outside, thunder rumbled again across the hills.

"You need to stop searching," the Bellboy continued calmly. "History is a fragile thing. Excessive attention tends to disturb the guests."

Tyler swallowed hard. "McKinney searched too, didn't he?"

For the first time, the Bellboy's smile faltered slightly. "Mr. McKinney became discourteous."

"He disappeared."

"He checked out."

Tyler stared at him in horror. The Bellboy took one slow step closer. "You misunderstand the Lodge entirely, sir. It is not punishment." His voice softened almost sympathetically. "It is invitation."

The overhead kitchen light flickered suddenly. For one split second, Tyler saw the Bellboy differently. Burned. Not burned like an accident victim. Burned black. Skin cracked open with glowing orange heat visible beneath it like furnace coals behind shattered porcelain. Then the image vanished. The Bellboy stood normal again. Smiling.

He nearly dropped the mug. "What are you?"

This time the Bellboy ignored the question entirely. Instead he nodded politely toward the front door. "You should leave for work soon," he said. "Traffic will be unpleasant this morning."

His breathing grew shallow. "You can't just come into my house."

"Oh, but I can, sir." The Bellboy's eyes drifted once more toward the jacket pocket containing the key. "You invited us."

The word hit hard. Invited. Checked in. Accepted hospitality. The Bellboy smiled faintly again. Then his expression cooled for the very first time. Not rage. Something worse. Disappointment.

"I would strongly advise against further research," he said quietly. "The Lodge dislikes being spoken of incorrectly."

The air temperature dropped sharply. He suddenly became aware of distant ballroom music drifting faintly through the house walls. The Bellboy stepped backward once. And vanished. No dramatic effect. No smoke. No flash of light. One second he stood beside the kitchen table. The next, the space sat empty. Only the faint smell of cigar smoke remained behind.

He stood frozen for nearly a full minute before finally forcing himself to move. His hands shook violently now. The ceramic mug slipped from his grip and shattered across the kitchen floor. He barely noticed.

Because resting neatly atop the kitchen table where the Bellboy had been sitting was an old black-and-white photograph. Walnut Lodge. June 11, 1930. And standing circled in dark ink near the ballroom entrance was Tyler himself.

Chapter 16

He stopped trusting reality by the end of the week. It wasn't a dramatic shift, more like a final step in a series of subtle alterations. Just enough that even ordinary moments brought hesitation. Every hallway. Every reflection. Every distant sound drifting through walls after midnight. He kept expecting the Lodge to appear around the next corner like fog rolling through trees.

And little by little, it did. The changes no longer stayed confined to dreams or brief flickers in his peripheral vision. The world itself had started bending around the edges.

On Thursday afternoon, he walked into the break room at work and found jazz music playing softly from an old tabletop radio sitting beside the microwave. The problem was nobody owned a radio. Amanda poured coffee only feet away, completely unbothered while muted trumpet music crackled through static behind her.

"You don't hear that?" He asked carefully.

"Hear what?"

"The music."

Amanda frowned at him. "Tyler, there's no music. You should get your hearing checked."

He looked back toward the counter. The radio was gone.

Later that evening, one of the warehouse elevators opened on a floor that didn't exist. He crossed the lobby when the doors slid apart on their own, revealing not the expected freight interior, but a narrow velvet hallway lit by chandeliers and candle sconces.

Walnut Lodge. The smell of cigar smoke and perfume rolled softly outward. Somewhere beyond the hallway, guests laughed. Then the doors shut again.

Nobody else even looked up. He spent the rest of the shift shaking at his desk. He couldn't stand the building by 5:00 that afternoon. He grabbed his coat, ignored Amanda asking if he was feeling alright, and headed toward the parking garage through cold evening rain.

The entire city looked wrong now. Downtown blurred beneath wet streets and glowing headlights while fog drifted low between buildings. Neon reflections shimmered across puddles like smeared oil paintings. Somewhere in the distance, thunder rolled softly over the mountains.

He kept checking mirrors while driving. Not because he feared traffic. Because he feared seeing the Bellboy. The realization alone nearly made him laugh from exhaustion.

He turned onto a narrow stretch of road outside downtown and allowed himself one slow breath. The car hummed steadily beneath him while windshield wipers pushed rain aside in rhythmic sweeps.

Then the passenger seat shifted. He froze. The Bellboy sat beside him. Perfectly calm. One pale hand rested atop his knee while rain-streaked highway lights flickered softly across his immaculate uniform.

He absently jerked violently against the steering wheel. The car swerved hard across the center line. "Oh God!"

The Bellboy didn't even blink. "You really should keep your eyes on the road, sir," he said pleasantly.

He slammed the brakes instinctively while tires screamed against wet pavement. Headlights whipped wildly through trees and guardrails as the car fishtailed sideways. "You're not here!"

The Bellboy smiled faintly. "An increasingly unconvincing position."

The car hydroplaned. He lost control instantly. The world spun sideways in flashes of rain, headlights, and screaming tires before the vehicle tore off the shoulder and crashed violently into a ditch.

Metal slammed hard enough to knock the breath from his lungs. The engine died. Silence followed. For several disoriented seconds, he simply sat there gripping the wheel while rain hammered the roof overhead.

Alive. Still alive. He looked slowly toward the passenger seat. Empty. Of course it was empty.

Steam hissed faintly from beneath the crumpled hood while he stumbled shakily from the vehicle into freezing rain. Mud sucked at his shoes beside the ditch while distant headlights approached through the storm.

By the time police arrived, he already rehearsed the lie. "Deer ran out in front of me," he explained while wrapped in a reflective blanket beside the road. "The car hydroplaned."

The officer nodded sympathetically. "Happens all the time up here."

He glanced once toward the dark tree line beyond the ditch. For one impossible second, the Bellboy stood there beneath the rain. Watching. Then lightning flashed overhead. The woods stood empty again.

The rental company delivered his temporary vehicle that evening while his damaged car went in for repairs. The representative chatted casually while handing over paperwork in the house driveway, completely oblivious to him barely listening. Because the world around them continued changing.

The house hallway looked longer now. Not dramatically. Just enough to be different. The walls seemed narrower too, covered faintly in patterns Tyler recognized from the Lodge wallpaper before returning to normal whenever he stared too hard.

The smells worsened as well. Smoke. Perfume. Champagne. Sometimes damp lake water. Other times the sharp stink of gas drifted suddenly through rooms before vanishing moments later. Worst of all were the sounds. The Lodge had grown louder.

Tyler heard distant ballroom music constantly now beneath ordinary life. Elevator cables groaned inside apartment walls. Soft laughter drifted through heating vents at night. Once he woke at three in the morning to the sound of guests applauding somewhere inside the house. And always, somewhere behind it all, came Thea's voice. *Return.*

But now he finally understood. Not return to the Lodge. Return the key. The realization settled fully into place sometime before dawn Friday morning while he sat sleepless at the kitchen table staring at the brass key beneath the overhead light.

Everything connected to it. The phone calls. The Bellboy. The manifestations. The Lodge wasn't following him randomly. The key had opened a door. And every day he kept it, the door widened.

He looked slowly around the house. The kitchen wallpaper had changed again. Only slightly. Dark burgundy vines curled faintly through the beige paint near the ceiling. A chandelier reflected dimly in the microwave door behind him. Somewhere deeper in the house, an elevator bell chimed softly.

Enough. He stood abruptly. Fear still lived inside him, heavy and cold, but exhaustion had finally burned through panic into something sharper. Resolve. He crossed the house quickly gathering supplies into his backpack. Flashlight. Water. Batteries. First-aid kit. The brass key. A handgun he hadn't touched in years but suddenly wanted nearby anyway.

Rain had finally stopped outside by sunrise. Fog drifted low across the mountains as pale morning light spread slowly over East Tennessee. He loaded the rental car silently while birds stirred through wet trees around the house.

The world looked ordinary again. Too ordinary. Like the Lodge was waiting. He slid behind the wheel and stared once toward the passenger seat before starting the engine. Empty. For now.

He backed slowly from the driveway and turned east toward Roan Mountain. Toward Walnut Lodge. Toward whatever waited beneath the mountain fog. This time he wasn't returning out of curiosity. He was going to end it.

Chapter 17

The mountain greeted him with fog. It rolled low between the trees in pale gray sheets as he parked near the abandoned trailhead just after sunrise. Cold air drifted through the forest carrying the scent of pine, wet earth, and distant rain. Somewhere high overhead, unseen birds called through the mist while the Appalachian wilderness stretched silent and endless around him. For a long moment, he sat behind the wheel and stared toward the trail. He tried to steady the unease twisting through his chest.

The place looked ordinary. No phantom ballroom lights glowed through the trees. No distant music drifted down from impossible windows high above the mountain. There was no sign of Walnut Lodge perched atop the summit waiting for him. Just wilderness, fog, and silence beneath a gray Tennessee morning.

That almost frightened him more. Tyler reached into his pocket and wrapped his fingers around the brass key. Instantly, a deep heaviness settled through his arm, dull and unnatural, like the weight of something much larger than a simple piece of metal. He frowned and pulled it free, turning it slowly beneath the weak morning light. The brass looked darker than before, the engraved lettering faintly warped along the edges.

It felt wrong. Not impossibly heavy. Not enough to defy logic outright. Just dense in a way metal shouldn't be dense, as though he held something tied to gravity differently than the rest of the world. He stepped from the rental car and immediately felt resistance pulling against him the closer he moved toward the trailhead.

The Lodge didn't want the key returned. The realization settled hard into his stomach as he started up the mountain path. Damp leaves shifted beneath his boots while fog curled through the trees in pale drifting ribbons. Every step seemed to make the key heavier in his hand, until his shoulder and wrist actually began to ache beneath the strain.

Then he heard footsteps behind him. He froze instantly. Silence followed for several seconds except for distant wind moving through the branches overhead. Then came another measured step somewhere beyond the fog, slow and deliberate, careful enough to sound almost polite. He swallowed hard and continued climbing.

The footsteps followed him. Never rushing. Never drawing closer. Just calmly keeping pace behind him somewhere among the trees. He didn't need to turn around to know who walked there. The mountain suddenly felt colder than before, the fog thicker and more suffocating around the narrow trail. "You should reconsider, sir," the Bellboy's voice drifted softly through the mist.

He kept walking without answering. The key dug heavily into his palm now, dragging against his arm like an anchor pulling backward toward the valley below. Sweat gathered cold beneath his jacket despite the mountain chill. Somewhere far away, faint ballroom music began stirring through the fog.

"You misunderstand the Lodge," the Bellboy called again. "It provided what you needed."

He laughed bitterly under his breath. The sound vanished quickly into the trees around him while dead leaves rustled beneath his boots. He tightened his grip on the key and forced himself onward through the rising fog.

"A haunted death trap?" he muttered.

"A refuge."

The answer echoed strangely through the woods. He paused. He hadn't thought of it in that way. No, no, it wasn't a refuge. It was a trap. He climbed another ridge and nearly stumbled as the weight of the key suddenly doubled in his hand. Pain shot sharply through his wrist while the brass surface burned ice cold against his skin.

The Bellboy spoke again, closer now. "She asked you to return because she belongs there. She wants you to belong there, too."

He finally stopped walking. Slowly, he turned toward the pale fog drifting between the trees behind him. The Bellboy stood motionless among the pines, his dark uniform almost blending into the shadows beneath the branches. He looked worse now.

Ash streaked the immaculate fabric of his coat while his pale skin appeared stretched too tightly across sharp cheekbones. Rain stains darkened the edges of his gloves and collar. Yet the smile remained exactly the same, fixed patiently across his face like something carved into stone.

"You don't belong there," he said quietly. The Bellboy tilted his head slightly as though considering the statement. Wind moved softly through the forest while distant music pulsed faintly somewhere deep inside the fog. Tyler could almost hear ballroom laughter beneath it now, muffled and far away.

"Everyone belongs somewhere." The Bellboy replied.

He stared at him for several long seconds. Then he turned away again and continued climbing toward the lake. This time, the footsteps did not immediately follow behind him. That unsettled him more than hearing them had.

By the time he reached the shoreline, his arm ached from carrying the key. Fog drifted low across the black water while pine trees loomed silently around the lake beneath the gray morning sky. The place looked exactly as it had in his dreams, ancient and still beneath the mountain mist. And resting near the water's edge lay the white Venetian mask.

Thea's mask sat half buried in wet leaves and mud beside the shoreline. The porcelain surface looked older now, stained darker by time and water. Cracks spread across one side while the ribbon ties had nearly rotted away completely. Yet somehow it still looked as though it had simply been waiting there for him to return.

He slowly crouched beside the lake. Cold wind moved across the water while the brass key pulled heavily against his arm. By now the thing felt nearly impossible to hold, as though the Lodge itself fought desperately to keep him from throwing it away. His wrist trembled visibly beneath the strain.

Behind him, the Bellboy spoke one final time. "If you do this, sir… the Lodge will forget you. You won't see her again."

He looked out across the still black water. Fog drifted slowly across the lake surface while distant mountains faded pale and ghostlike beyond the shoreline. For the first time since leaving Walnut Lodge, he felt truly exhausted rather than frightened.

"That's the idea," he said softly. Then he threw the key into the lake. The instant it struck the water, the mountain screamed. The sound erupted from everywhere at once, a shrieking metallic howl that tore violently through the forest and shook the trees themselves. The lake churned beneath the fog while wind exploded outward across the shoreline in spiraling gusts. Somewhere deep beneath the water, Tyler heard elevator cables snapping and ballroom glass shattering in rapid succession.

Then came the roar of fire. For one terrible moment, Walnut Lodge appeared reflected across the lake surface in full blazing ruin. Flames burst from shattered windows while smoke billowed into the mountain sky. Guests screamed behind glowing ballroom curtains while the Bellboy stood at the front entrance burning black beneath the firelight. And for the first time, he was no longer smiling.

Then the reflection collapsed.

Silence crashed down across the mountain almost instantly. The water stilled beneath the fog while the forest settled into quiet once more. He stood frozen near the shoreline breathing hard as cold wind moved softly through the trees around him.

After several long moments, he finally looked down again. The Venetian mask was gone. So were the strange reflections in the lake. The lingering smell of smoke had vanished from the mountain air. Even the faint distant music that haunted the forest since his first visit had disappeared completely.

Only the lake remained. Still. Quiet. Ordinary beneath the pale morning sky. Tyler slowly turned toward the trees surrounding the shoreline. The Bellboy was gone too. For the first time in days, the mountain felt empty.

Not haunted. Not waiting. Just old and silent beneath drifting Appalachian fog. Birds stirred again somewhere high in the branches while sunlight slowly began breaking through the clouds overhead.

Normal sounds. Real sounds. He lowered himself carefully onto a nearby rock and stared out across the lake while the morning grew brighter around him. No one would ever believe what happened here. No police report or newspaper article would explain the things he'd seen inside Walnut Lodge.

The place would survive only as fragments. A plaque on a forgotten mountain trail. Contradictory newspaper archives buried in old libraries. Missing hikers and ghost stories whispered beside campfires late at night. And somewhere beneath all of it, hidden forever beneath fog and memory, the dead would finally rest. At least, rest as peacefully as possible.

He rose slowly and adjusted the backpack on his shoulder. Morning sunlight filtered warmly through the trees now while the fog continued lifting from the lake. He looked once more across the still water, then turned and started down the mountain toward home. This time, nothing followed him.

ABOUT THE AUTHOR

L. Chambers Wright writes the kind of Southern Gothic fiction that lingers in your bones long after the last page. Her stories thread the uncanny through the everyday, with haunted houses, forgotten cemeteries, and long-silent typewriters that sometimes still have something to say. Set deep in the Appalachian mountains, her novels explore grief, inheritance, and the thin places where memory and myth meet.

Known for her atmospheric prose and slow-burning dread, Wright conjures the weight of legacy and the cost of keeping secrets. These are stories where curses move like blood through a family line, where lost sisters don't always stay gone, and where the woods aren't just dark—they're listening.

Other Works:

As Laura Wright

- *The Girl in the Trees*
- *Kinnie Wagner (The History of Bad Men)*
- *Appalachian Curiosities*
- *Bizarre TriCities*
- *Timeslips & Terrors*

As L. Chambers Wright

- *Infectious*
- *The Demon Machine*
- *The Moon Sees Me*
- *Moonshine*
- *Stormy Weather*
- *The Bad Room*

www.ingramcontent.com/pod-product-compliance
Lightning Source LLC
LaVergne TN
LVHW091012080826
845145LV00003B/1239

9781967310463